The Straw

Eugene O'Neill

Alpha Editions

This edition published in 2024

ISBN : 9789362992024

Design and Setting By
Alpha Editions
www.alphaedis.com
Email - info@alphaedis.com

Contents

ACT ONE
ACT ONE: SCENE ONE

The kitchen of the Carmody home on the outskirts of a manufacturing town in Connecticut. On the left, forward, the sink. Farther back, two windows looking out on the yard. In the left corner, rear, the icebox. Immediately to the right of it, in the rear wall, a window opening on the side porch. To the right of this, a china cupboard, and a door leading into the hall where the main front entrance to the house and the stairs to the floor above are situated. On the right, to the rear, a door opening on to the dining room. Further forward, the kitchen range with scuttle, wood box, etc. In the centre of the room, a table with a red and white cloth. Four cane-bottomed chairs are pushed under the table. In front of the stove, two battered wicker rocking chairs. The floor is partly covered by linoleum strips. The walls are papered a light cheerful colour. Several old framed picture-supplement prints hang from nails. Everything has a clean, neatly-kept appearance. The supper dishes are piled in the sink ready for washing. A saucepan of water simmers on the stove.

It is about eight o'clock in the evening of a bitter cold day in late February of the year 1912.

As the curtain rises, Bill Carmody is discovered fitting in a rocker by the stove, reading a newspaper and smoking a blackened clay pipe. He is a man of fifty, heavy-set and round-shouldered, with long muscular arms and swollen-veined, hairy hands. His face is bony and ponderous; his nose short and squat; his mouth large, thick-lipped and harsh; his complexion mottled—red, purple-streaked, and freckled; his hair, short and stubby with a bald spot on the crown. The expression of his small, blue eyes is one of selfish cunning. His voice is loud and hoarse. He wears a flannel shirt, open at the neck, criss-crossed by red braces; black, baggy trousers grey with dust; muddy brogues.

His youngest daughter, Mary, is sitting on a chair by the table, front, turning over the pages of a picture book. She is a delicate, dark-haired, blue-eyed, quiet little girl about eight years old.

CARMODY (after watching the child's preoccupation for a moment, in a tone of half exasperated amusement). Well, but you're the quiet one, surely! (Mary looks up at him with a shy smile, her eyes still full of dreams.) Glory be to God, I'd not know a soul was alive in the room, barrin' myself. What is it you're at, Mary, that there's not a word out of you?

MARY. I'm looking at the pictures.

CARMODY. It's the dead spit and image of your sister Eileen you are, with your nose always in a book; and you're like your mother, too, God rest her soul. (He crosses himself with pious unction and Mary also does so.) It's Nora and Tom has the high spirits in them like their father; and Billy, too,—if he is a lazy, shiftless divil—has the fightin' Carmody blood like me. You're a Cullen like your mother's people. They always was dreamin' their lives out. (He lights his pipe and shakes his head with ponderous gravity.) There's no good in too many books, I'll tell you. It's out rompin' and playin' with your brother and sister you ought to be at your age, not carin' a fig for books. (With a glance at the clock.) Is that auld fool of a doctor stayin' the night? If he had his wits about him he'd know in a jiffy 'tis only a cold has taken Eileen, and give her the medicine. Run out in the hall, Mary, and see if you hear him. He may have sneaked away by the front door.

MARY (goes out into the hall, rear, and comes back). He's upstairs. I heard him talking to Eileen.

CARMODY. Close the door, ye little divil! There's a freezin' draught comin' in. (She does so and comes back to her chair. Carmody continues with a sneer.) It's mad I am to be thinkin' he'd go without gettin' his money—the like of a doctor! (Angrily.) Rogues and thieves they are, the lot of them, robbin' the poor like us! I've no use for their drugs at all. They only keep you sick to pay more visits. I'd not have sent for this bucko if Eileen didn't scare me by faintin'.

MARY (anxiously). Is Eileen very sick, Papa?

CARMODY (spitting—roughly). If she is, it's her own fault entirely—weakenin' her health by readin' here in the house. This'll be a lesson for her, and for you, too. (Irritably.) Put down that book on the table and leave it be. I'll have no more readin' in this house, or I'll take the strap to you!

MARY (laying the book on the table). It's only pictures.

CARMODY. No back talk! Pictures or not, it's all the same mopin' and lazin' in it. (After a pause—morosely.) It's the bad luck I've been havin' altogether this last year since your mother died. Who's to do the work and look after Nora and Tom and yourself, if Eileen is bad took and has to stay in her bed? I'll have to get Mrs. Brennan come look after the house. That means money, too, and where's it to come from? All that I've saved from slavin' and sweatin' in the sun with a gang of lazy Dagoes'll be up the spout in no time. (Bitterly.) What a fool a man is to be raisin' a raft of children and him not a millionaire! (With lugubrious self-pity.) Mary, dear, it's a black curse God put on me when he took your mother just when I needed her most. (Mary commences to sob. Carmody starts and looks at her angrily.) What are you sniffin' at?

MARY (tearfully). I was thinking—of Mamma.

CARMODY (scornfully). It's late you are with your tears, and her cold in her grave for a year. Stop it, I'm tellin' you! (Mary gulps back her sobs.)

(There is a noise of childish laughter and screams from the street in front. The outside door is opened and slammed, footsteps pound along the hall. The door in the rear is pushed open, and Nora and Tom rush in breathlessly. Nora is a bright, vivacious, red-haired girl of eleven—pretty after an elfish, mischievous fashion—light-hearted and robust.)

(Tom resembles Nora in disposition and appearance. A healthy, good-humoured youngster with a shock of sandy hair. He is a year younger than Nora. They are followed into the room, a moment later, by their brother Billy, who is evidently loftily disgusted with their antics. Billy is a fourteen-year-old replica of his father, whom he imitates even to the hoarse, domineering tone of voice.)

CARMODY (grumpily). Ah, here you are, the lot of you. Shut that door after you! What's the use in me spendin' money for coal if all you do is to let the cold night in the room itself?

NORA (hopping over to him—teasingly). Me and Tom had a race, Papa. I beat him. (She sticks her tongue out at her younger brother.) Slow poke!

TOM. You didn't beat me, neither!

NORA. I did, too!

TOM. You did not! You didn't play fair. You tripped me comin' up the steps. Brick-top! Cheater!

NORA (flaring up). You're a liar! You stumbled over your own big feet, clumsy bones! And I beat you fair Didn't I, Papa?

CARMODY (with a grin). You did, darlin', and fair, too. (Tom slinks back to the chair in the rear of table, sulking. Carmody pats Nora's red hair with delighted pride.) Sure it's you can beat the divil himself!

NORA (sticks out her tongue again at Tom). See? Liar! (She goes and perches on the table near Mary, who is staring sadly in front of her.)

CARMODY (to Billy—irritably). Did you get the plug for me I told you?

BILLY. Sure. (He takes a plug of tobacco from his pocket and hands it to his father. Nora slides down off her perch and disappears, unnoticed, under the table.)

CARMODY. It's a great wonder you didn't forget it—and me without a chew. (He bites off a piece and tucks it into his cheek.)

TOM (suddenly clutching at his leg with a yell). Ouch! Darn you! (He kicks frantically at something under the table, but Nora scrambles out at the other end, grinning.)

CARMODY (angrily). Shut your big mouth! What is the matter with you at all?

TOM (indignantly). She pinched me—hard as she could, too—and look at her laughin'!

NORA (hopping on the table again). Cry-baby! I owed you one.

TOM. I'll fix you. I'll tell Eileen, wait 'n' see!

NORA. Tattle-tale! I don't care. Eileen's sick.

TOM. That's why you dast do it. You dasn't if she was up. I'll get even, you bet!

CARMODY (exasperated). Shut up your noise! Go up to bed, the two of you, and no more talk, and you go with them, Mary.

NORA (giving a quick tug at Mary's hair). Come on, Mary. Wake up.

MARY. Ow! (She begins to cry.)

CARMODY (raising his voice furiously). Hush your noise, you soft, weak thing, you! It's nothin' but blubberin' you do be doin' all the time. (He stands up threateningly.) I'll have a moment's peace, I will! Off to bed with you before I get the strap! It's crazy mad you all get the moment Eileen's away from you. Go on, now! (They scurry out of the rear door.) And be quiet or I'll be up to you!

NORA (sticks her head back in the door). Can I say good-night to Eileen, Papa?

CARMODY. No. The doctor's with her yet. (Then he adds hastily.) Yes, go in to her, Nora. It'll drive himself out of the house maybe, bad cess to him, and him stayin' half the night. (Nora waits to hear no more but darts back, shutting the door behind her. Billy takes the chair in front of the table. Carmody sits down again with a groan.) The rheumatics are in my leg again. (Shakes his head.) If Eileen's in bed long those brats'll have the house down.

BILLY. Eileen ain't sick very bad, is she?

CARMODY (easily). It's a cold only she has. (Then mournfully.) Your poor mother died of the same. (Billy looks awed.) Ara, well, it's God's will, I suppose, but where the money'll come from, I dunno. (With a disparaging glance at his son.) They'll not be raisin' your wages soon, I'll be bound.

BILLY (surlily). Naw. The old boss never gives no one a raise, 'less he has to. He's a tight-wad for fair.

CARMODY (still scanning him with contempt). Five dollars a week—for a strappin' lad the like of you! It's shamed you should be to own up to it. A divil of a lot of good it was for me to go against Eileen's wish and let you leave off your schoolin' this year like you wanted, thinkin' the money you'd earn at work would help with the house.

BILLY. Aw, goin' to school didn't do me no good. The teachers was all down on me. I couldn't learn nothin' there.

CARMODY (disgustedly). Nor any other place, I'm thinkin', you're that thick, (There is a noise from the stairs in the hall.) Whisht! It's the doctor comin' down from Eileen. What'll he say, I wonder? (The door in the rear is opened and Doctor Gaynor enters. He is a stout, bald, middle-aged man, forceful of speech, who in the case of patients of the Carmodys' class dictates rather than advises. Carmody adopts a whining tone.) Aw, Doctor, and how's Eileen now? Have you got her cured of the weakness?

GAYNOR (does not answer this but comes forward into the room holding out two slips of paper—dictatorially). Here are two prescriptions that'll have to be filled immediately.

CARMODY (frowning). You take them, Billy, and run round to the drug store. (Gaynor hands them to Billy.)

BILLY. Give me the money, then.

CARMODY (reaches down into his trousers pocket with a sigh). How much will they come to, Doctor?

GAYNOR. About a dollar, I guess.

CARMODY (protestingly). A dollar! Sure it's expensive medicines you're givin' her for a bit of a cold. (He meets the doctor's cold glance of contempt and he wilts—grumblingly, as he peels a dollar bill off a small roll and gives it to Billy.) Bring back the change—if there is any. And none of your tricks, for I'll stop at the drug store myself to-morrow and ask the man how much it was.

BILLY. Aw, what do you think I am? (He takes the money and goes out.)

CARMODY (grudgingly). Take a chair, Doctor, and tell me what's wrong with Eileen.

GAYNOR (seating himself by the table—gravely). Your daughter is very seriously ill.

CARMODY (irritably). Aw, Doctor, didn't I know you'd be sayin' that, anyway!

GAYNOR (ignoring this remark—coldly). Your daughter has tuberculosis of the lungs.

CARMODY (with puzzled awe). Too-ber-c'losis?

GAYNOR. Consumption, if that makes it plainer to you.

CARMODY (with dazed terror—after a pause). Consumption? Eileen? (With sudden anger.) What lie is it you're tellin' me?

GAYNOR (icily). Look here, Carmody! I'm not here to stand for your insults!

CARMODY (bewilderingly). Don't be angry, now, at what I said. Sure I'm out of my wits entirely. Eileen to have the consumption! Ah, Doctor, sure you must be mistaken!

GAYNOR. There's no chance for a mistake, I'm sorry to say. Her right lung is badly affected.

CARMODY (desperately). It's a bad cold only, maybe.

GAYNOR (curtly). Don't talk nonsense. (Carmody groans. Gaynor continues authoritatively.) She will have to go to a sanatorium at once. She ought to have been sent to one months ago. The girl's been keeping up on her nerve when she should have been in bed, and it's given the disease a chance to develop. (Casts a look of indignant scorn at Carmody, who is sitting staring at the floor with an expression of angry stupor on his face.) It's a wonder to me you didn't see the condition she was in and force her to take care of herself. Why, the girl's nothing but skin and bone!

CARMODY (with vague fury). God blast it!

GAYNOR. No, your kind never realises things till the crash comes—usually when it's too late. She kept on doing her work, I suppose—taking care of her brothers and sisters, washing, cooking, sweeping, looking after your comfort—worn out—when she should have been in bed—and—— (He gets to his feet with a harsh laugh.) But what's the use of talking? The damage is done. We've got to set to work to repair it at once. I'll write to-night to Dr. Stanton of the Hill Farm Sanatorium and find out if he has a vacancy. And if luck is with us we can send her there at once. The sooner the better.

CARMODY (his face growing red with rage). Is it sendin' Eileen away to a hospital you'd be? (Exploding.) Then you'll not! You'll get that notion out of your head damn quick. It's all nonsense you're stuffin' me with, and lies, makin' things out to be the worst in the world. I'll not believe a word of Eileen having the consumption at all. It's doctors' notions to be always lookin' for a sickness that'd kill you. She'll not move a step out of here, and I say so, and I'm her father!

GAYNOR (who has been staring at him with contempt—coldly angry). You refuse to let your daughter go to a sanatorium?

CARMODY. I do.

GAYNOR (threateningly). Then I'll have to report her case to the Society for the Prevention of Tuberculosis of this county, and tell them of your refusal to help her.

CARMODY (wavering a bit). Report all you like, and be damned to you!

GAYNOR (ignoring the interruption—impressively). A majority of the most influential men of this city are behind the Society. Do you know that? (Grimly.) We'll find a way to move you, Carmody, if you try to be stubborn.

CARMODY (thoroughly frightened, but still protesting). Ara, Doctor, you don't see the way of it at all. If Eileen goes to the hospital, who's to be takin' care of the others, and mindin' the house when I'm off to work?

GAYNOR. You can easily hire some woman.

CARMODY (at once furious again). Hire? D'you think I'm a millionaire itself?

GAYNOR (contemptuously). That's where the shoe pinches, eh? (In a rage.) I'm not going to waste any more words on you, Carmody, but I'm damn well going to see this thing through! You might as well give in first as last.

CARMODY (wailing). But where's the money comin' from?

GAYNOR (brutally). That's your concern. Don't lie about your poverty. You've a steady well-paid job, and plenty of money to throw away on drunken sprees, I'll bet. The weekly fee at the Hill Farm is only seven dollars. You can easily afford that—the price of a few rounds of drinks.

CARMODY. Seven dollars! And I'll have to pay a woman to come in—and the four of the children eatin' their heads off! Glory be to God, I'll not have a penny saved for me old age—and then it's the poor-house!

GAYNOR (curtly). Don't talk nonsense!

CARMODY. Ah, doctor, it's the truth I'm tellin' you!

GAYNOR. Well, perhaps I can get the Society to pay half for your daughter—if you're really as hard up as you pretend. They're willing to do that where it seems necessary.

CARMODY (brightening). Ah, Doctor, thank you.

GAYNOR (abruptly). Then it's all settled?

CARMODY (grudgingly—trying to make the best of it). I'll do my best for Eileen, if it's needful—and you'll not be tellin' them people about it at all, Doctor?

GAYNOR. Not unless you force me to.

CARMODY. And they'll pay the half, surely?

GAYNOR. I'll see what I can do—for your daughter's sake, not yours, understand!

CARMODY. God bless you, Doctor! (Grumblingly.) It's the whole of it they ought to be payin', I'm thinkin', and them with bags of money. 'Tis them builds the hospitals and why should they be wantin' the poor like me to support them?

GAYNOR (disgustedly). Bah! (Abruptly.) I'll telephone to Doctor Stanton to-morrow morning. Then I'll know something definite when I come to see your daughter in the afternoon.

CARMODY (darkly). You'll be comin' again tomorrow? (Half to himself.) Leave it to the likes of you to be drainin' a man dry.

(Gaynor has gone out to the hall in rear and does not hear this last remark. There is a loud knock from the outside door. The Doctor comes back into the room carrying his hat and overcoat.)

GAYNOR. There's someone knocking.

CARMODY. Who'll it be? Ah, it's Fred Nicholls, maybe. (In a low voice to Gaynor who has started to put on his overcoat.) Eileen's young man, Doctor, that she's engaged to marry, as you might say.

GAYNOR (thoughtfully). H'mm—yes—she spoke of him.

(As another knock sounds Carmody hurries to the rear. Gaynor, after a moments indecision, takes off his overcoat again and sits down. A moment later Carmody re-enters, followed by Fred Nicholls, who has left his overcoat and hat in the hallway. Nicholls is a young fellow of twenty-three, stockily built, fair-haired, handsome in a commonplace, conventional mould. His manner is obviously an attempt at suave gentility; he has an easy, taking smile and a ready laugh, but there is a petty, calculating expression in his small, observing, blue eyes. His well-fitting, ready-made clothes are carefully pressed. His whole get-up suggests an attitude of man-about-small-town complacency.)

CARMODY (as they enter). I had a mind to phone to your house, but I wasn't wishful to disturb you, knowin' you'd be comin' to call to-night.

NICHOLLS (with disappointed concern). It's nothing serious, I hope.

CARMODY (grumblingly). Ah, who knows? Here's the doctor. You've not met him?

NICHOLLS (politely, looking at Gaynor, who inclines his head stiffly). I haven't had the pleasure. Of course, I've heard——

CARMODY. It's Doctor Gaynor. This is Fred Nicholls, Doctor. (The two men shake hands with conventional greetings.) Sit down, Fred, that's a good lad, and be talkin' to the Doctor a moment while I go upstairs and see how is Eileen. She's all alone up there.

NICHOLLS. Certainly, Mr. Carmody. Go ahead—and tell her how sorry I am to learn she's under the weather.

CARMODY. I will so. (He goes out.)

GAYNOR (after a pause in which he is studying Nicholls). Do you happen to be any relative to the Albert Nicholls who is superintendent over at the Downs Manufacturing Company?

NICHOLLS (smiling). He's sort of a near relative—my father.

GAYNOR. Ah, yes?

NICHOLLS (with satisfaction). I work for the Downs Company myself—bookkeeper——

GAYNOR. Miss Carmody—the sick girl upstairs—she had a position there also, didn't she, before her mother died?

NICHOLLS. Yes. She had a job as stenographer for a time. When she graduated from the business college course—I was already working at the Downs—and through my father's influence—you understand. (Gaynor nods curtly.) She was getting on finely, too, and liked the work. It's too bad—her mother's death, I mean—forcing her to give it up and come home to take care of those kids.

GAYNOR. It's a damn shame. That's the main cause of her breakdown.

NICHOLLS (frowning). I've noticed she's been looking badly lately. So that's the trouble? Well, it's all her father's fault—and her own, too, because whenever I raised a kick about his making a slave of her, she always defended him. (With a quick glance at the Doctor—in a confidential tone.) Between us, Carmody's as selfish as they make 'em, if you want my opinion.

GAYNOR (with a growl). He's a hog on two legs.

NICHOLLS (with a gratified smile). You bet! (With a patronising air.) I hope to get Eileen away from all this as soon as—things pick up a little. (Making haste to explain his connection with the dubious household.) Eileen and I have gone around together for years—went to Grammar and High School together—in different classes, of course. She's really a corker—very different from the rest of the family you've seen—like her mother. She's really educated and knows a lot—used to carry off all the prizes at school. My folks like her awfully well. Of course, they'd never stand for—him.

GAYNOR. You'll excuse my curiosity—I've a good reason for it—but you and Miss Carmody are engaged, aren't you? Carmody said you were.

NICHOLLS (embarrassed). Why, yes, in a way—but nothing definite—no official announcement or anything of that kind. It's all in the future. We have to wait, you know. (With a sentimental smile.) We've been sort of engaged for years, you might say. It's always been sort of understood between us. (He laughs awkwardly.)

GAYNOR (gravely). Then I can be frank with you. I'd like to be because I may need your help. I don't put much faith in any promise Carmody makes. Besides, you're bound to know anyway. She'd tell you.

NICHOLLS (a look of apprehension coming over his face). Is it—about her sickness?

GAYNOR. Yes.

NICHOLLS. Then—it's serious?

GAYNOR. It's pulmonary tuberculosis—consumption.

NICHOLLS (stunned). Consumption? Good heavens! (After a dazed pause—lamely.) Are you sure, Doctor?

GAYNOR. Positive. (Nicholls stares at him with vaguely frightened eyes.) It's had a good start—thanks to her father's blind selfishness—but let's hope that can be overcome. The important thing is to ship her off to a sanatorium immediately. Carmody wouldn't hear of it at first. However, I managed to bully him into consenting; but I don't trust his word. That's where you can be of help. It's up to you to convince him that it's imperative she be sent away at once—for the safety of those around her as well as her own.

NICHOLLS (confusedly). I'll do my best, Doctor. (As if he couldn't yet believe his ears—shuddering!) Good heavens! She never said a word about—being so ill. She's had a cold. But, Doctor—do you think this sanatorium will——?

GAYNOR (with hearty hopefulness). Most certainly. She has every chance. The Hill Farm has a really surprising record of arrested cases—as good as any place in the country. Of course, she'll never be able to live as carelessly as before, even after the most favourable results. She'll have to take care of herself. (Apologetically.) I'm telling you all this as being the one most intimately concerned. I don't count Carmody. You are the one who will have to assume responsibility for her welfare when she returns to everyday life.

NICHOLLS (answering as if he were merely talking to screen the thoughts in his mind). Yes—certainly. Where is this sanatorium, Doctor—very far away?

GAYNOR. Half an hour by train to the town. The sanatorium is two miles out on the hills—a nice drive. You'll be able to see her whenever you've a day off. It's a pleasant trip.

NICHOLLS (a look of horrified realisation has been creeping into his eyes). You said—Eileen ought to be sent away—for the sake of those around her——?

GAYNOR. That's obvious. T.B. is extremely contagious, you must know that. Yet I'll bet she's been fondling and kissing those brothers and sisters of hers regardless. (Nicholls fidgets uneasily on his chair.) And look at this house sealed tight against the fresh air! Not a window open an inch! (Fuming.) That's what we're up against in the fight with T.B.—a total ignorance of the commonest methods of prevention——

NICHOLLS (his eyes shiftily avoiding the doctor's face). Then the kids might have gotten it—by kissing Eileen?

GAYNOR. It stands to reason that's a common means of communication.

NICHOLLS (very much shaken). Yes. I suppose it must be. But that's terrible, isn't it? (With sudden volubility, evidently extremely anxious to wind up this conversation and conceal his thoughts from Gaynor.) I'll promise you, Doctor, I'll tell Carmody straight what's what. He'll pay attention to me or I'll know the reason why.

GAYNOR (getting to his feet and picking up his overcoat). Good boy! You've probably saved me a disagreeable squabble. I won't wait for Carmody. The sight of him makes me lose my temper. Tell him I'll be back to-morrow with definite information about the sanatorium.

NICHOLLS (helping him on with his overcoat, anxious to have him go). All right, Doctor.

GAYNOR (puts on his hat). And do your best to cheer the patient up when you talk to her. Give her confidence in her ability to get well. That's half the battle. And she'll believe it, coming from you.

NICHOLLS (hastily). Yes, yes, I'll do all I can.

GAYNOR (turns to the door and shakes Nicholls' hand sympathetically). And don't take it to heart too much yourself. There's every hope, remember that. In six months she'll come back to you her old self again.

NICHOLLS (nervously). It's hard on a fellow—so suddenly—but I'll remember—and—— (Abruptly). Good night, Doctor.

GAYNOR. Good night.

(He goes out. The outer door is heard shutting behind him. Nicholls closes the door, rear, and comes back and sits in the chair in front of table. He rests his chin on his hands and stares before him, a look of desperate, frightened calculation coming into his eyes. Carmody is heard clumping heavily down the stairs. A moment later he enters. His expression is glum and irritated.)

CARMODY (coming forward to his chair by the stove). Has he gone away?

NICHOLLS (turning on him with a look of repulsion). Yes. He told me to tell you he'd be back to-morrow with definite information—about the sanatorium business.

CARMODY (darkly). Oho, he did, did he? Maybe I'll surprise him. I'm thinkin' it's lyin' he is about Eileen's sickness, and her lookin' as fresh as a daisy with the high colour in her cheeks when I saw her now.

NICHOLLS (impatiently). That's silly, Mr. Carmody. Gaynor knows his business. (After a moment's hesitation.) He told me all about Eileen's sickness.

CARMODY (resentfully). Did he now, the auld monkey! Small thanks to him to be tellin' our secrets to the town.

NICHOLLS (exasperated). I didn't want to learn your affairs. He only told me because you'd said I and Eileen were engaged. You're the one who was telling—secrets.

CARMODY (irritated). Ara, don't be talkin'! That's no secret at all with the whole town watchin' Eileen and you spoonin' together from the time you was kids.

NICHOLLS (vindictively). Well, the whole town is liable to find out—— (He checks himself.)

CARMODY (too absorbed in his own troubles to notice this threat). To hell with the town and all in it! I've troubles enough of my own. So he told you he'd send Eileen away to the hospital? I've half a mind not to let him—and let him try to make me! (With a frown.) But Eileen herself says she's wantin' to go, now. (Angrily.) It's all that divil's notion he put in her head that the children'd be catchin' her sickness that makes her willin' to go.

NICHOLLS (with a superior air). From what he told me, I should say it was the only thing for Eileen to do if she wants to get well quickly. (Spitefully.) And I'd certainly not go against Gaynor, if I was you. He told me he'd make it hot for you if you did. He will, too, you can bet on that. He's that kind.

CARMODY (worriedly). He's a divil. But what can he do—him and his Sasiety? I'm her father.

NICHOLLS (seeing Carmody's uneasiness, with revengeful satisfaction). Oh, he'll do what he says, don't worry! You'll make a mistake if you think he's bluffing. It'd probably get in all the papers about you refusing. Every one would be down on you. (As a last jab—spitefully.) You might even lose your job over it, people would be so sore.

CARMODY (jumping to his feet). Ah, divil take him! Let him send her where he wants, then. I'll not be sayin' a word.

NICHOLLS (as an afterthought). And, honestly, Mr. Carmody, I don't see how you can object for a second—after he's told you it's absolutely necessary for Eileen to go away. (Seeing Carmody's shaken condition, he finishes boldly.) You've some feeling for your own daughter, haven't you? You'd be a fine father if you hadn't!

CARMODY (apprehensively). Whisht! She might hear you. But you're right. Let her do what she's wishful to, and get well soon.

NICHOLLS (complacently—feeling his duty in the matter well done). That's the right spirit. I knew you'd see it that way. And you and I'll do all we can to help her. (He gets to his feet.) Well, I guess I'll have to go. Tell Eileen——

CARMODY. You're not goin'? Sure, Eileen is puttin' on her clothes to come down and have a look at you. She'll be here in a jiffy. Sit down now, and wait for her.

NICHOLLS (suddenly panic-stricken by the prospect of facing her). No—no—I can't stay—I only came for a moment—I've got an appointment—

honestly. Besides, it isn't right for her to be up. She's too weak. It'll make her worse. You should have told her.

(The door in the rear is opened and Eileen enters. She is just over eighteen. Her wavy mass of dark hair is parted in the middle and combed low on her forehead, covering her ears, to a knot at the back of her head. The oval of her face is spoiled by a long, rather heavy Irish jaw contrasting with the delicacy of her other features. Her eyes are large and blue, confident in their compelling candour and sweetness; her lips, full and red, half-open over strong, even teeth, droop at the corners into an expression of wistful sadness; her clear complexion is unnaturally striking in its contrasting colours, rose and white; her figure is slight and undeveloped. She wears a plain black dress with a bit of white at the neck and wrists. She stands looking appealingly at Nicholls, who avoids her glance. Her eyes have a startled, stunned expression as if the doctor's verdict were still in her ears.)

EILEEN (faintly—forcing a smile). Good evening, Fred. (Her eyes search his face anxiously.)

NICHOLLS (confusedly). Hello, Eileen. I'm so sorry to—— (Clumsily trying to cover up his confusion, he goes over and leads her to a chair.) You must sit down. You've got to take care of yourself. You never ought to have got up to-night.

EILEEN (sits down). I wanted to talk to you. (She raises her face with a pitiful smile. Nicholls hurriedly moves back to his own chair.)

NICHOLLS (almost brusquely). I could have talked to you from the hall. You're silly to take chances just now.

(Eileen's eyes show her hurt at his tone.)

CARMODY (seeing his chance—hastily). You'll be stayin' a while now, Fred? I'll take a walk down the road. I'm needin' a drink to clear my wits. (He goes to the door in rear.)

EILEEN (reproachfully). You won't be long, Father? And please don't—you know.

CARMODY (exasperated). Sure who wouldn't get drunk with all the sorrows of the world piled on him? (He stamps out. A moment later the outside door bangs behind him. Eileen sighs. Nicholls walks up and down with his eyes on the floor.)

NICHOLLS (furious at Carmody for having left him in this situation). Honestly, Eileen, your father is the limit. I don't see how you stand for him. He's the most selfish——

EILEEN (gently). Sssh! You mustn't, Fred. He's not to blame. He just doesn't understand. (Nicholls snorts disdainfully.) Don't! Let's not talk about him now. We won't have many more evenings together for a long, long time. Did father or the Doctor tell you—— (She falters.)

NICHOLLS (not looking at her—glumly). Everything there was to tell, I guess.

EILEEN (hastening to comfort him). You mustn't worry, Fred. Please don't! It'd make it so much worse for me if I thought you did. I'll be all right. I'll do exactly what they tell me, and in a few months I'll be back so fat and healthy you won't know me.

NICHOLLS (lamely). Oh, there's no doubt of that. No one's worrying about your not getting well quick.

EILEEN. It won't be long. We can write often, and it isn't far away. You can come out and see me every Sunday—if you want to.

NICHOLLS (hastily). Of course I will!

EILEEN (looking at his face searchingly). Why do you act so funny? Why don't you sit down—here, by me? Don't you want to?

NICHOLLS (drawing up a chair by hers—flushing guiltily). I—I'm all flustered, Eileen. I don't know what I'm doing.

EILEEN (putting her hand on his knee). Poor Fred! I'm so sorry I have to go. I didn't want to at first. I knew how hard it would be on father and the kids—especially little Mary. (Her voice trembles a bit.) And then the doctor said if I stayed I'd be putting them all in danger. He even ordered me not to kiss them any more. (She bites her lip to restrain a sob—then coughs, a soft, husky cough. Nicholls shrinks away from her to the edge of his chair, his eyes shifting nervously with fright. Eileen continues gently.) So I've got to go and get well, don't you see?

NICHOLLS (wetting his dry lips). Yes—it's better.

EILEEN (sadly). I'll miss the kids so much. Taking care of them has meant so much to me since mother died. (With a half-sob she suddenly throws her arms about his neck and hides her face on his shoulder. He shudders and fights against an impulse to push her away.) But I'll miss you most of all, Fred. (She lifts her lips towards his, expecting a kiss. He seems about to kiss her—then averts his face with a shrinking movement, pretending he hasn't seen. Eileen's eyes grow wide with horror. She throws herself back into her chair, staring accusingly at Nicholls. She speaks chokingly.) Fred! Why—why didn't you kiss—what is it? Are you—afraid? (With a moaning sound.) Oooh!

NICHOLLS (goaded by this accusation into a display of manhood, seizes her fiercely by the arms). No! What—what d'you mean? (He tries to kiss her, but she hides her face.)

EILEEN (in a muffled voice of hysterical self-accusation, pushing his head away). No, no, you mustn't! I was wrong. The doctor told you not to, didn't he? Please don't, Fred! It would be awful if anything happened to you—through me. (Nicholls gives up his attempts, recalled to caution by her words. She raises her face and tries to force a smile through her tears.) But you can kiss me on the forehead, Fred. That can't do any harm. (His face crimson, he does so. She laughs hysterically.) It seems so silly—being kissed that way—by you. (She gulps back a sob and continued to attempt to joke.) I'll have to get used to it, won't I?

THE CURTAIN FALLS

ACT ONE: SCENE TWO.

The reception room of the Infirmary, a large, high-ceilinged room painted white, with oiled, hard wood floor. In the left wall, forward, a row of four windows. Farther back, the main entrance from the drive, and another window. In the rear wall left, a glass partition looking out on the sleeping porch. A row of white beds, with the faces of patients barely peeping out from under piles of heavy bed-clothes, can be seen. To the right of this partition, a bookcase, and a door leading to the hall past the patients' rooms. Farther right, another door opening on the examining room. In the right wall, rear, a door to the office. Farther forward, a row of windows. In front of the windows, a long dining-table with chairs. On the left of the table, towards the centre of the room, a chimney with two open fire-places, facing left and right. Several wicker armchairs are placed around the fire-place on the left in which a cheerful wood fire is crackling. To the left of centre, a round reading and writing table with a green-shaded electric lamp. Other electric lights are in brackets around the walls. Easy chairs stand near the table, which is stacked with magazines. Rocking chairs are placed here and there about the room, near the windows, etc. A gramophone stands near the left wall, forward.

It is nearing eight o'clock of a cold evening about a week later.

At the rise of the curtain Stephen Murray is discovered sitting in a chair in front of the fireplace, left. Murray is thirty years old—a tall, slender, rather unusual-looking fellow with a pale face, sunken under high cheek bones, lined about the eyes and mouth, jaded and worn for one still so young. His intelligent, large hazel eyes have a tired, dispirited expression in repose, but can quicken instantly with a concealed mechanism of mocking, careless humour whenever his inner privacy is threatened. His large mouth aids this process of protection by a quick change from its set apathy to a cheerful grin of cynical good nature. He gives off the impression of being somehow dissatisfied with himself, but not yet embittered enough by it to take it out on others. His manner, as revealed by his speech—nervous, inquisitive, alert—seems more an acquired quality than any part of his real nature. He stoops a trifle, giving him a slightly round-shouldered appearance. He is dressed in a shabby dark suit, baggy at the knees. He is staring into the fire, dreaming, an open book lying unheeded on the arm of his chair. The gramophone is whining out the last strains of Dvorak's Humoresque. In the doorway to the office, Miss Gilpin stands talking to Miss Howard. The former is a slight, middle-aged woman with black hair, and a strong, intelligent face, its expression of resolute efficiency softened and made kindly by her warm, sympathetic grey eyes. Miss Howard is tall, slender and blonde—decidedly pretty and provokingly conscious of it, yet with a certain air of seriousness underlying her apparent frivolity. She is twenty years old. The elder woman is dressed in the all-white of a full-fledged nurse. Miss Howard wears the grey-blue uniform of one still in training. The record finishes. Murray sighs with relief, but makes no move to get up and stop the grinding needle. Miss Howard hurries across to the machine. Miss Gilpin goes back into the office.

MISS HOWARD (takes off the record, glancing at Murray with amused vexation). It's a wonder you wouldn't stop this machine grinding itself to bits, Mr. Murray.

MURRAY (with a smile). I was hoping the darn thing would bust. (Miss Howard sniffs. Murray grins at her teasingly.) It keeps you from talking to me. That's the real music.

MISS HOWARD (comes over to his chair laughing). It's easy to see you've got Irish in you. Do you know what I think? I think you're a natural born kidder. All newspaper reporters are like that, I've heard.

MURRAY. You wrong me terribly. (Then frowning.) And it isn't charitable to remind me of my job. I hoped to forget all about it up here.

MISS HOWARD (surprised). I think it's great to be able to write. I wish I could. You ought to be proud of it.

MURRAY (glumly). I'm not. You can't call it writing—not what I did—small town stuff. (Changing the subject.) But I wanted to ask you something. Do you know when I'm to be moved away to the huts?

MISS HOWARD. In a few days, I guess. Don't be impatient. (Murray grunts and moves nervously on his chair.) What's the matter? Don't you like us here at the Sanatorium?

MURRAY (smiling). Oh—you—yes! (Then seriously.) I don't care for the atmosphere, though. (He waves his hand towards the partition looking out on the porch.) All those people in bed out there on the porch seem so sick. It's depressing. I can't do anything for them—and—it makes me feel so helpless.

MISS HOWARD. Well, it's the rules, you know. All the patients have to come here first until Doctor Stanton finds out whether they're well enough to be sent out to the huts and cottages. And remember you're a patient just like the ones in bed out there—even if you are up and about.

MURRAY. I know it. But I don't feel as I were—really sick like them.

MISS HOWARD (wisely). None of them do, either.

MURRAY (after a moment's reflection—cynically). Yes, I suppose it's that pipe dream that keeps us all going, eh?

MISS HOWARD. Well, you ought to be thankful. You're very lucky, if you knew it. (Lowering her voice.) Shall I tell you a secret? I've seen your chart and you've no cause to worry. Doctor Stanton joked about it. He said you were too uninteresting—there was so little the matter with you.

MURRAY (pleased, but pretending indifference). Humph! He's original in that opinion.

MISS HOWARD. I know it's hard your being the only one up the week since you've been here, with no one to talk to; but there's another patient due to-day. Maybe she'll be well enough to be around with you. (With a quick glance at her wrist watch.) She can't be coming unless she got in on the last train.

MURRAY (interestedly). It's a she, eh?

MISS HOWARD. Yes.

MURRAY (grinning provokingly). Young?

MISS HOWARD. Eighteen, I believe. (Seeing his grin—with feigned pique.) I suppose you'll be asking if she's pretty next! Oh, you men are all alike, sick or well. Her name is Carmody, that's the only other thing I know. So there!

MURRAY. Carmody?

MISS HOWARD. Oh, you don't know her. She's from another part of the state from your town.

MISS GILPIN (appearing in the office doorway). Miss Howard.

MISS HOWARD. Yes, Miss Gilpin. (In an aside to Murray as she leaves him.) It's time for those horrid diets.

(She hurries back into the office. Murray stares into the fire. Miss Howard reappears from the office and goes out by the door to the hall, rear. Carriage wheels are heard from the drive in front of the house on the left. They stop. After a pause there is a sharp rap on the door and a bell rings insistently. Men's muffled voices are heard in argument. Murray turns curiously in his chair. Miss Gilpin comes from the office and walks quickly to the door, unlocking and opening it. Eileen enters, followed by Nicholls, who is carrying her suit-case, and by her father.)

EILEEN. I'm Miss Carmody. I believe Doctor Gaynor wrote——

MISS GILPIN (taking her hand—with kind affability). We've been expecting you all day. How do you do? I'm Miss Gilpin. You came on the last train, didn't you?

EILEEN (heartened by the other woman's kindness). Yes. This is my father, Miss Gilpin—and Mr. Nicholls.

(Miss Gilpin shakes hands cordially with the two men who are staring about the room in embarrassment. Carmody has very evidently been drinking. His voice is thick and his face puffed and stupid. Nicholls' manner is that of one who is accomplishing a necessary but disagreeable duty with the best grace possible, but is frightfully eager to get it over and done with. Carmody's condition embarrasses him acutely and when he glances at him it is with hatred and angry disgust.)

MISS GILPIN (indicating the chairs in front of the windows on the left, forward). Won't you gentlemen sit down? (Carmody grunts sullenly and plumps himself into the one nearest the door. Nicholls hesitates, glancing down at the suit-case he carries. Miss Gilpin turns to Eileen.) And now we'll get you settled immediately. Your room is all ready for you. If you'll follow me—— (She turns toward the door in rear, centre.)

EILEEN. Let me take the suit-case now, Fred.

MISS GILPIN (as he is about to hand it to her—decisively). No, my dear, you mustn't. Put the case right down there, Mr. Nicholls. I'll have it taken to Miss Carmody's room in a moment. (She shakes her finger at Eileen with kindly admonition.) That's the first rule you'll have to learn. Never exert yourself or tax your strength. It's very important. You'll find laziness is a virtue instead of a vice with us.

EILEEN (confused). I—I didn't know——

MISS GILPIN (smiling). Of course you didn't. And now if you'll come with me I'll show you your room. We'll have a little chat there and I can explain all the other important rules in a second. The gentlemen can make themselves comfortable in the meantime. We won't be gone more than a moment.

NICHOLLS (feeling called upon to say something). Yes—we'll wait—certainly, we're all right.

(Carmody remains silent, glowering at the fire. Nicholls sits down beside him. Miss Gilpin and Eileen go out. Murray switches his chair so that he can observe the two men out of the corner of his eye while pretending to be absorbed in his book.)

CARMODY (looking about shiftily and reaching for the inside pocket of his overcoat). I'll be havin' a nip now we're alone, and that cacklin' hen gone. I'm feelin' sick in the pit of the stomach. (He pulls out a pint flask, half full.)

NICHOLLS (excitedly). For God's sake, don't! Put that bottle away! (In a whisper.) Don't you see that fellow in the chair there?

CARMODY (taking a big drink). Ah, I'm not mindin' a man at all. Sure I'll bet it's himself would be likin' a taste of the same. (He appears about to get up and invite Murray to join him, but Nicholls grabs his arm.)

NICHOLLS (with a frightened look at Murray who appears buried in his book). Stop it, you—— Don't you know he's probably a patient and they don't allow them——

CARMODY (scornfully). A sick one, and him readin' a book like a dead man without a civil word out of him! It's queer they'd be allowin' the sick ones to read books, when I'll bet it's the same lazy readin' in the house brought the half of them down with the consumption itself. (Raising his voice.) I'm thinking this whole shebang is a big, thievin' fake—and I've always thought so.

NICHOLLS (furiously). Put that bottle away, damn it! And don't shout. You're not in a public-house.

CARMODY (with provoking calm). I'll put it back when I'm ready, not before, and no lip from you!

NICHOLLS (with fierce disgust). You're drunk now. It's disgusting.

CARMODY (raging). Drunk, am I? Is it the like of a young jackass like you that's still wet behind the ears to be tellin' me I'm drunk?

NICHOLLS (half-rising from his chair—pleadingly). For heaven's sake, Mr. Carmody, remember where we are and don't raise any rumpus. What'll Eileen say? Do you want to make trouble for her at the start?

CARMODY (puts the bottle away hastily, mumbling to himself—then glowers about the room scornfully with blinking eyes). It's a grand hotel this is, I'm thinkin', for the rich to be takin' their ease, and not a hospital for the poor, but the poor has to pay for it.

NICHOLLS (fearful of another outbreak). Sssh!

CARMODY. Don't be shshin' at me? I'm tellin' you the truth. I'd make Eileen come back out of this to-night if that divil of a doctor didn't have me by the throat.

NICHOLLS (glancing at him nervously). I wonder how soon she'll be back? The carriage is waiting for us. We'll have to hurry to make that last train back. If we miss it—it means two hours on the damn tram.

CARMODY (angrily). Is it anxious to get out of her sight you are, and you engaged to marry and pretendin' to love her? (Nicholls flushes guiltily. Murray pricks up his ears and stares over at Nicholls. The latter meets his glance, scowls, and hurriedly averts his eyes. Carmody goes on accusingly.) Sure, it's no heart at all you have—and her your sweetheart for years—and her sick with the consumption—and you wild to run away from her and leave her alone.

NICHOLLS (springing to his feet—furiously). That's a——! (He controls himself with an effort. His voice trembles.) You're not responsible for the idiotic things you're saying or I'd—— (He turns away, seeking some escape from the old man's tongue.) I'll see if the man is still there with the carriage. (He walks to the door on left and goes out.)

CARMODY (following him with his eyes). Go to hell, for all I'm preventin'. You've got no guts of a man in you. (He addresses Murray with the good nature inspired by the flight of Nicholls.) Is it true you're one of the consumptives, young fellow?

MURRAY (delighted by this speech—with a grin). Yes, I'm one of them.

CARMODY. My name's Carmody. What's yours, then?

MURRAY. Murray.

CARMODY (slapping his thigh). Irish as Paddy's pig! (Murray nods. Carmody brightens and grows confidential.) I'm glad to be knowin' you're one of us. You can keep an eye on Eileen. That's my daughter that came with us. She's got consumption like yourself.

MURRAY. I'll be glad to do all I can.

CARMODY. Thanks to you—though it's a grand life she'll be havin' here from the fine look of the place. (With whining self-pity.) It's me it's hard on, God help me, with four small children and me widowed, and havin' to hire a woman to come in and look after them and the house now that Eileen's sick; and payin' for her curin' in this place, and me with only a bit of money in the bank for my old age. That's hard, now, on a man, and who'll say it isn't?

MURRAY (made uncomfortable by this confidence). Hard luck always comes in bunches. (To head off Carmody who is about to give vent to more woe—quickly, with a glance towards the door from the hall.) If I'm not mistaken, here comes your daughter now.

CARMODY (as Eileen comes into the room). I'll make you acquainted. Eileen! (She comes over to them, embarrassed to find her father in his condition so chummy with a stranger. Murray rises to his feet.) This is Mr. Murray, Eileen. I want you to meet. He's Irish and he'll put you on to the ropes of the place. He's got the consumption, too, God pity him.

EILEEN (distressed). Oh, Father, how can you—— (With a look at Murray which pleads for her father.) I'm glad to meet you, Mr. Murray.

MURRAY (with a straight glance at her which is so frankly admiring that she flushes and drops her eyes). I'm glad to meet you. (The front door is opened and Nicholls re-appears, shivering with the cold. He stares over at the others with ill-concealed irritation.)

CARMODY (noticing him—with malicious satisfaction). Oho, here you are again. (Nicholls scowls and turns away. Carmody addresses his daughter with a sly wink at Murray.) I thought Fred was slidin' down hill to the train with his head bare to the frost, and him so desperate hurried to get away from here. Look at the knees on him clappin' together with the cold, and with the great fear that's in him he'll be catchin' a sickness in this place! (Nicholls, his guilty conscience stabbed to the quick, turns pale with impotent rage.)

EILEEN (remonstrating pitifully). Father! Please! (She hurries over to Nicholls.) Oh, please don't mind him, Fred. You know what he is when he's drinking. He doesn't mean a word he's saying.

NICHOLLS (thickly). That's all right—for you to say. But I won't forget—I'm sick and tired standing for—I'm not used to—such people.

EILEEN (shrinking from him). Fred!

NICHOLLS (with a furious glance at Murray). Before that cheap slob, too—letting him know everything!

EILEEN (faintly). He seems—very nice.

NICHOLLS. You've got your eyes set on him already, have you? Leave it to you! No fear of your not having a good time of it out here!

EILEEN. Fred!

NICHOLLS. Well, go ahead if you want to. I don't care. I'll—— (Startled by the look of anguish which comes over her face, he hastily swallows his words. He takes out his watch—fiercely.) We'll miss that train, damn it!

EILEEN (in a stricken tone). Oh, Fred! (Then forcing back her tears she calls to Carmody in a strained voice.) Father! You'll have to go now. Miss Gilpin told me to tell you you'd have to go right away to catch the train.

CARMODY (shaking hands with Murray). I'll be goin'. Keep your eye on her. I'll be out soon to see her and you and me'll have another talk.

MURRAY. Glad to. Good-bye for the present. (He walks to windows on the far right, turning his back considerately on their leave-taking.)

EILEEN (comes to Carmody and hangs on his arm as they proceed to the door). Be sure and kiss them all for me—Billy and Tom and Nora and little Mary—and bring them out to see me as soon as you can, father, please! And you come often, too, won't you? And don't forget to tell Mrs. Brennan all the directions I gave you coming out on the train. I told her, but she mightn't remember—about Mary's bath—and to give Tom his——

CARMODY (impatiently). Hasn't she brought up brats of her own, and doesn't she know the way of it? Don't be worryin' now, like a fool.

EILEEN (helplessly). Never mind telling her, then. I'll write to her.

CARMODY. You'd better not. Leave her alone. She'll not wish you mixin' in with her work and tellin' her how to do it.

EILEEN (aghast). Her work! (She seems at the end of her tether—wrung too dry for any further emotion. She kisses her father at the door with indifference and speaks calmly.) Good-bye, father.

CARMODY (in a whining tone of injury). A cold kiss! And never a small tear out of her! Is your heart a stone? (Drunken tears well from his eyes and he blubbers.) And your own father going back to a lone house with a stranger in it!

EILEEN (wearily, in a dead voice). You'll miss your train, father.

CARMODY (raging in a second). I'm off, then! Come on, Fred. It's no welcome we have with her here in this place—and a great curse on this day I brought her to it! (He stamps out.)

EILEEN (in the same dead tone). Good-bye, Fred.

NICHOLLS (repenting his words of a moment ago—confusedly). I'm sorry, Eileen—for what I said. I didn't mean—you know what your father is—excuse me, won't you?

EILEEN (without feeling). Yes.

NICHOLLS. And I'll be out soon—in a week if I can make it. Well then,—good-bye for the present. (He bends down as if to kiss her, but she shrinks back out of his reach.)

EILEEN (a faint trace of mockery in her weary voice). No, Fred. Remember you mustn't now.

NICHOLLS (in an instant huff). Oh, if that's the way you feel about——

(He strides out and slams the door viciously behind him. Eileen walks slowly back towards the fire-place, her face fixed in a dead calm of despair. As she sinks into one of the armchairs, the strain becomes too much. She breaks down, hiding her face in her hands, her frail shoulders heaving with the violence of her sobs. At this sound, Murray turns from the windows and comes over near her chair.)

MURRAY (after watching her for a moment—in an embarrassed tone of sympathy). Come on, Miss Carmody, that'll never do. I know it's hard at first—but—getting yourself all worked up is bad for you. You'll run a temperature and then they'll keep you in bed—which isn't pleasant. Take hold of yourself! It isn't so bad up here—really—once you get used to it! (The shame she feels at giving way in the presence of a stranger only adds to her loss of control and she sobs heartbrokenly. Murray walks up and down nervously, visibly nonplussed and upset. Finally he hits upon something.) One of the nurses will be in any minute. You don't want them to see you like this.

EILEEN (chokes back her sobs and finally raises her face and attempts a smile). I'm sorry—to make such a sight of myself. I just couldn't help it.

MURRAY (jocularly). Well, they say a good cry does you a lot of good.

EILEEN (forcing a smile). I do feel—better.

MURRAY (staring at her with a quizzical smile—cynically). You shouldn't take those lovers' squabbles so seriously. To-morrow he'll be sorry—you'll be sorry. He'll write begging forgiveness—you'll do ditto. Result—all serene again.

EILEEN (a shadow of pain on her face—with dignity). Don't—please.

MURRAY (angry at himself—hanging his head contritely). I'm a fool. Pardon me. I'm rude sometimes—before I know it. (He shakes off his confusion with a renewed attempt at a joking tone.) You can blame your father for any breaks I make. He made me your guardian, you know—told me to see that you behaved.

EILEEN (with a genuine smile). Oh, father! (Flushing.) You mustn't mind anything he said to-night.

MURRAY (thoughtlessly). Yes, he was well lit up. I envied him. (Eileen looks very shame-faced. Murray sees it and exclaims in exasperation at himself.) Darn! There I go again putting my foot in it! (With an irrepressible grin.) I ought to have my tongue operated on—that's what's the matter with me. (He laughs and throws himself in a chair.)

EILEEN (forced in spite of herself to smile with him). You're candid, at any rate, Mr. Murray.

MURRAY. Don't misunderstand me. Far be it from me to cast slurs at your father's high spirits. I said I envied him his jag and that's the truth. The same candour compels me to confess that I was pickled to the gills myself when I arrived here. Fact! I made love to all the nurses and generally disgraced myself—and had a wonderful time.

EILEEN. I suppose it does make you forget your troubles—for a while.

MURRAY (waving this aside). I didn't want to forget—not for a second. I wasn't drowning my sorrow. I was hilariously celebrating.

EILEEN (astonished—by this time quite interested in this queer fellow to the momentary forgetfulness of her own grief). Celebrating—coming here? But—aren't you sick?

MURRAY. T.B.? Yes, of course. (Confidentially.) But it's only a matter of time when I'll be all right again. I hope it won't be too soon. I was dying for a rest—a good, long rest with time to think about things. I'm due to get what I wanted here. That's why I celebrated.

EILEEN (with wide eyes). I wonder if you really mean——

MURRAY. What I've been sayin'? I sure do—every word of it!

EILEEN (puzzled). I can't understand how anyone could—— (With a worried glance over her shoulder.) I think I'd better look for Miss Gilpin, hadn't I? She may wonder—— (She half rises from her chair.)

MURRAY (quickly). No. Please don't go yet. Sit down. Please do. (She glances at him irresolutely, then resumes her chair.) They'll give you your diet of milk and shoo you off to bed on that freezing porch soon enough, don't worry. I'll see to it that you don't fracture any rules. (Hitching his chair nearer hers—impulsively.) In all charity to me you've got to stick awhile. I haven't had a chance to really talk to a soul for a week. You found what I said a while ago hard to believe, didn't you?

EILEEN (with a smile). Isn't it? You said you hoped you wouldn't get well too soon!

MURRAY. And I meant it! This place is honestly like heaven to me—a lonely heaven till your arrival. (Eileen looks embarrassed.) And why wouldn't it be? I've no fear for my health—eventually. Just let me tell you what I was getting away from—— (With a sudden laugh full of a weary bitterness.) Do you know what it means to work from seven at night till three in the morning as a reporter on a morning newspaper in a town of twenty thousand people—for ten years? No. You don't. You can't. No one could who hadn't been through the mill. But what it did to me—it made me happy—yes, happy!—to get out here—T.B. and all, notwithstanding.

EILEEN (looking at him curiously). But I always thought being a reporter was so interesting.

MURRAY (with a cynical laugh). Interesting? On a small town rag? A month of it, perhaps, when you're a kid and new to the game. But ten years. Think of it! With only a raise of a couple of dollars every blue moon or so, and a weekly spree on Saturday night to vary the monotony. (He laughs again.) Interesting, eh? Getting the dope on the Social of the Queen Esther Circle in the basement of the Methodist Episcopal Church, unable to sleep through a meeting of the Common Council on account of the noisy oratory caused by John Smith's application for a permit to build a house; making a note that a tugboat towed two barges loaded with coal up the river, that Mrs. Perkins spent a week-end with relatives in Hickville, that John Jones—— Oh help! Why go on? Ten years of it! I'm a broken man. God, how I used to pray that our Congressman would commit suicide, or the Mayor murder his wife—just to be able to write a real story!

EILEEN (with a smile). Is it as bad as that? But weren't there other things in the town—outside your work—that were interesting?

MURRAY (decidedly). No. Never anything new—and I knew everyone and every thing in town by heart years ago. (With sudden bitterness.) Oh, it was my own fault. Why didn't I get out of it? Well, I didn't. I was always going to—to-morrow—and to-morrow never came. I got in a rut—and stayed put. People seem to get that way, somehow—in that town. It's in the air. All the boys I grew up with—nearly all, at least—took root in the same way. It took pleurisy, followed by T.B., to blast me loose.

EILEEN (wonderingly). But—your family—didn't they live there?

MURRAY. I haven't much of a family left. My mother died when I was a kid. My father—he was a lawyer—died when I was nineteen, just about to go to college. He left nothing, so I went to work on the paper instead. And there I've been ever since. I've two sisters, respectably married and living in another part of the state. We don't get along—but they are paying for me here, so I suppose I've no kick. (Cynically.) A family wouldn't have changed things. From what I've seen that blood-thicker-than-water dope is all wrong. It's thinner than table-d'hôte soup. You may have seen a bit of that truth in your own case already.

EILEEN (shocked). How can you say that? You don't know——

MURRAY. Don't I, though? Wait till you've been here three months or four—when the gap you left has been comfortably filled. You'll see then!

EILEEN (angrily, her lips trembling). You must be crazy to say such things! (Fighting back her tears.) Oh, I think it's hateful—when you see how badly I feel!

MURRAY (in acute confusion. Stammering). Look here, Miss Carmody, I didn't mean to—— Listen—don't feel mad at me, please. My tongue ran away with me. I was only talking. I'm like that. You mustn't take it seriously.

EILEEN (still resentful). I don't see how you can talk. You don't—you can't know about these things—when you've just said you had no family of your own, really.

MURRAY (eager to return to her good graces). No. Of course I don't know. I was just talking regardless for the fun of listening to it.

EILEEN (after a pause). Hasn't either of your sisters any children?

MURRAY. One of them has—two of them—ugly, squally little brats.

EILEEN (disapprovingly). You don't like babies?

MURRAY (bluntly). No. (Then with a grin at her shocked face.) I don't get them. They're something I can't seem to get acquainted with.

EILEEN (with a smile, indulgently). You're a funny person. (Then with a superior, motherly air.) No wonder you couldn't understand how badly I feel. (With a tender smile.) I've four of them—my brothers and sisters—though they're not what you'd call babies, except to me. Billy is fourteen, Nora eleven, Tom ten, and even little Mary is eight. I've been a mother to them now for a whole year—ever since our mother died (Sadly.) And I don't know how they'll ever get along while I'm away.

MURRAY (cynically). Oh, they'll—(He checks what he was going to say and adds lamely)—get along somehow.

EILEEN (with the same superior tone). It's easy for you to say that. You don't know how children grow to depend on you for everything. You're not a woman.

MURRAY (with a grin). Are you? (Then with a chuckle.) You're as old as the pyramids, aren't you? I feel like a little boy. Won't you adopt me, too?

EILEEN (flushing, with a shy smile). Someone ought to. (Quickly changing the subject.) Do you know, I can't get over what you said about hating your work so. I should think it would be wonderful—to be able to write things.

MURRAY. My job had nothing to do with writing. To write—really write—yes, that's something worth trying for. That's what I've always meant to have a stab at. I've run across ideas enough for stories—that sounded good to me, anyway. (With a forced, laugh.) But—like everything else—I never got down to it. I started one or two—but—either I thought I didn't have the time or—— (He shrugs his shoulders.)

EILEEN. Well, you've plenty of time now, haven't you?

MURRAY (instantly struck by this suggestion). You mean—I could write—up here? (She nods. His face lights up with enthusiasm.) Say! That is an idea! Thank you! I'd never have had sense enough to have thought of that myself. (Eileen flushes with pleasure.) Sure there's time—nothing but time up here——

EILEEN. Then you seriously think you'll try it?

MURRAY (determinedly). Yes. Why not? I've got to try and do something real some time, haven't I? I've no excuse not to, now. My mind isn't sick.

EILEEN (excitedly). That'll be wonderful!

MURRAY (confidently). Listen. I've had ideas for a series of short stories for the last couple of years—small town experiences, some of them actual. I know that life—too darn well. I ought to be able to write about it. And if I can sell one—to the Post, say—I'm sure they'd take the others, too. And then—I should worry! It'd be easy sailing. But you must promise to help—play critic for me—read them and tell me where they're rotten.

EILEEN (pleased, but protesting). Oh, no, I'd never dare. I don't know anything——

MURRAY. Yes, you do. You're the public. And you started me off on this thing—if I'm really starting at last. So you've got to back me up now. (Suddenly.) Say, I wonder if they'd let me have a typewriter up here?

EILEEN. It'd be fine if they would. I'd like to have one, too—to practice. I learned stenography at a business college and then I had a position for a year—before my mother died.

MURRAY. We could hire one—I could. I don't see why they wouldn't allow it. I'm to be sent to one of the men's huts within the next few days, and you'll be shipped to one of the women's cottages within ten days. You're not sick enough to be kept here in bed, I'm sure of that.

EILEEN. I—I don't know——

MURRAY. Here! None of that! You just think you're not and you won't be. Say, I'm keen on that typewriter idea. They couldn't kick if we only used it during recreation periods. I could have it a week, and then you a week.

EILEEN (eagerly). And I could type your stories after you've written them! I could help that way.

MURRAY (smiling). But I'm quite able—— (Then seeing how interested she is he adds hurriedly.) That'd be great! It'd save so much time. I've always been a fool at a machine. And I'd be willing to pay whatever—— (Miss Gilpin enters from the rear and walks towards them.)

EILEEN (quickly). Oh, no! I'd be glad to get the practice. I wouldn't accept—— (She coughs slightly.)

MURRAY (with a laugh). Maybe, after you've read my stuff, you won't type it at any price.

MISS GILPIN. Miss Carmody, may I speak to you for a moment, please.

(She takes Eileen aside and talks to her in low tones of admonition. Eileen's face falls. She nods a horrified acquiescence. Miss Gilpin leaves her and goes into the office, rear.)

MURRAY (as Eileen comes back. Noticing her perturbation. Kindly). Well? Now, what's the trouble?

EILEEN (her lips trembling). She told me I mustn't forget to shield my mouth with my handkerchief when I cough.

MURRAY (consolingly). Yes, that's one of the rules, you know.

EILEEN (falteringly). She said they'd give me—a—cup to carry around— (She stops, shuddering.)

MURRAY (easily). It's not as horrible as it sounds. They're only little paste-board things you carry in your pocket.

EILEEN (as if speaking to herself). It's so horrible (She holds out her hand to Murray.) I'm to go to my room now. Good night, Mr. Murray.

MURRAY (holding her hand for a moment—earnestly). Don't mind your first impressions here. You'll look on everything as a matter of course in a few days. I felt your way at first. (He drops her hand and shakes his finger at her.) Mind your guardian, now! (She forces a trembling smile.) See you at breakfast. Good night.

(Eileen goes out to the hall in rear. Miss Howard comes in from the door just after her, carrying a glass of milk.)

MISS HOWARD. Almost bedtime, Mr. Murray. Here's your diet. (He takes the glass. She smiles at him provokingly.) Well, is it love at first sight, Mr. Murray?

MURRAY (with a grin). Sure thing! You can consider yourself heartlessly jilted. (He turns and raises his glass towards the door through which Eileen has just gone, as if toasting her.)

"A glass of milk, and thou

Coughing beside me in the wilderness—

Ah—wilderness were Paradise enow!"

(He takes a sip of milk.)

MISS HOWARD (peevishly). That's old stuff, Mr. Murray. A patient at Saranac wrote that parody.

MURRAY (maliciously). Aha, you've discovered it's a parody, have you, you sly minx! (Miss Howard turns from him huffily and walks back towards the office, her chin in the air.)

THE CURTAIN FALLS

ACT TWO
ACT TWO: SCENE ONE

The assembly room of the main building of the sanatorium—early in the morning of a fine day in June, four months later. The room is large, light and airy, painted a fresh white. On the left forward, an armchair. Farther back, a door opening on the main hall. To the rear of this door, a pianola on a raised platform. At back of the pianola, a door leading into the office. In the rear wall, a long series of French windows looking out on the lawn, with wooded hills in the far background. Shrubs in flower grow immediately outside the windows Inside, there is a row of potted plants. In the right wall, rear, four windows. Farther forward, a long well-filled bookcase, and a doorway leading into the dining-room. Following the walls, but about five feet out from them a stiff line of chairs placed closely against each other forms a sort of right-angled auditorium of which the large, square table that stands at centre, forward, would seem to be the stage.

From the dining-room comes the clatter of dishes, the confused murmur of many voices, male and female—all the mingled sounds of a crowd of people at a meal.

After the curtain rises, Doctor Stanton enters from the hall, followed by a visitor, Mr. Sloan, and the assistant physician, Doctor Simms. Doctor Stanton is a handsome man of forty-five or so with a grave, care-lined, studious face lightened by a kindly, humorous smile. His grey eyes, saddened by the suffering they have witnessed, have the sympathetic quality of real understanding. The look they give is full of companionship, the courage-renewing, human companionship of a hope which is shared. He speaks with a slight Southern accent, soft and slurring. Doctor Simms is a tall, angular young man with a long sallow face and a sheepish, self-conscious grin. Mr. Sloan is fifty, short and stout, well dressed—one of the successful business men whose endowments have made the Hill Farm a possibility.

STANTON (as they enter). This is what you might see in the general assembly room, Mr. Sloan—where the patients of both sexes are allowed to congregate together after meals, for diets, and in the evening.

SLOAN (looking around him). Couldn't be more pleasant, I must say—light and airy. (He walks to where he can take a peep into the dining-room.) Ah, they're all at breakfast, I see.

STANTON (smiling). Yes, and with no lack of appetite, let me tell you. (With a laugh of proud satisfaction.) They'd sure eat us out of house and home at one sitting, if we'd give them the opportunity. (To his assistant.) Wouldn't they, Doctor?

SIMMS (with his abashed grin). You bet they would, sir.

SLOAN (with a smile). That's fine. (With a nod towards the dining-room.) The ones in there are the sure cures, aren't they?

STANTON (a shadow coming over his face). Strictly speaking, there are no sure cures in this disease, Mr. Sloan. When we permit a patient to return to take up his or her activities in the world, the patient is what we call an arrested case. The disease is overcome, quiescent; the wound is healed over. It's then up to the patient to so take care of himself that this condition remains permanent. It isn't hard for them to do this, usually. Just ordinary, bull-headed common sense—added to what they've learned here—is enough for their safety. And the precautions we teach them to take don't diminish their social usefulness in the slightest, either, as I can prove by our statistics of former patients. (With a smile.) It's rather early in the morning for statistics, though.

SLOAN (with a wave of the hand). Oh, you needn't. Your reputation in that respect, Doctor—— (Stanton inclines his head in acknowledgment. Sloan jerks his thumb towards the dining-room.) But the ones in there are getting well, aren't they?

STANTON. To all appearances, yes. You don't dare swear to it, though. Sometimes, just when a case looks most favourably, there's a sudden, unforeseen breakdown, and they have to be sent back to bed, or, if it's very serious, back to the Infirmary again. These are the exceptions, however, not the rule. You can bank on most of those eaters being out in the world and usefully employed within six months.

SLOAN. You couldn't say more than that (Abruptly.) But—the unfortunate ones—do you have many deaths?

STANTON (with a frown). No. We're under a very hard, almost cruel imperative which prevents that. If, at the end of six months, a case shows no response to treatment, continues to go down hill—if, in a word, it seems hopeless—we send them away, to one of the State Farms if they have no private means. (Apologetically.) You see, this sanatorium is overcrowded and has a long waiting list, most of the time, of others who demand their chance for life. We have to make places for them. We have no time to waste on incurables. There are other places for them—and sometimes, too, a change is beneficial and they pick up in new surroundings. You never can tell. But we're bound by the rule. It may seem cruel—but it's as near justice to all concerned as we can come.

SLOAN (soberly). I see. (His eyes fall on the pianola in surprise.) Ah—a piano.

STANTON (replying to the other's thought). Yes, some patients play and sing. (With a smile.) If you'd call the noise they make by those terms. They'd dance, too, if we permitted it. There's only one big taboo—Home, Sweet Home. We forbid that—for obvious reasons.

SLOAN. I see. (With a final look around.) Did I understand you to say this is the only place where the sexes are permitted to mingle?

STANTON. Yes, sir.

SLOAN (with a smile). Not much chance for a love affair then.

STANTON (seriously). We do our best to prevent them. We even have a strict rule which allows us to step in and put a stop to any intimacy which grows beyond the casual. People up here, Mr. Sloan, are expected to put aside all ideas except the one—getting well.

SLOAN (somewhat embarrassed). A damn good rule, too, I should say, under the circumstances.

STANTON (with a laugh). Yes, we're strictly anti-Cupid, sir, from top to bottom, (Turning to the door to the hall.) And now, if you don't mind, Mr. Sloan, I'm going to turn you loose to wander about the grounds on an unconducted tour. To-day is my busy morning—Saturday. We weigh each patient immediately after breakfast.

SLOAN. Every week?

STANTON. Every Saturday. You see we depend on fluctuations in weight to tell us a lot about the patient's condition. If they gain, or stay at normal, all's usually well. If they lose week after week without any reason we can definitely point to, we keep careful watch. It's a sign that something's wrong. We're forewarned by it and on our guard.

SLOAN (with a smile). Well, I'm certainly learning things. (He turns to the door.) And you just shoo me off wherever you please and go on with the good work. I'll be glad of a ramble in the open on such a glorious morning.

STANTON. After the weighing is over, sir, I'll be free to——

(His words are lost as the three go out. A moment later, Eileen enters from the dining-room. She has grown stouter, her face has more of a healthy, out-of-door colour, but there is still about her the suggestion of being worn down by a burden too oppressive for her courage. She is dressed in blouse and dark skirt. She goes to the armchair, left forward, and sinks down on it. She is evidently in a state of nervous depression; she twists her fingers together in her lap; her eyes stare sadly before her; she clenches her upper lip with her teeth to prevent its trembling. She has hardly regained control over herself when Stephen Murray comes in hurriedly from the dining-room and, seeing her at his first glance, walks quickly over to her chair. He is the picture of health, his figure has filled out solidly, his tanned face beams with suppressed exultation.)

MURRAY (excitedly). Eileen! I saw you leave your table. I've something to tell you. I didn't get a chance last night after the mail came. You'd gone to the cottage. Just listen, Eileen—it's too good to be true—but on that mail—guess what?

EILEEN (forgetting her depression—with an excited smile). I know! You've sold your story!

MURRAY (triumphantly). Go to the head of the class. What d'you know about that for luck! My first, too—and only the third magazine I sent it to! (He cuts a joyful caper.)

EILEEN (happily). Isn't that wonderful, Stephen! But I knew all the time you would. The story's so good.

MURRAY. Well, you might have known, but I didn't think there was a chance in the world. And as for being good—(With superior air)—wait till I turn loose with the real big ones, the kind I'm going to write. Then I'll make them sit up and take notice. They can't stop me now. This money gives me a chance to sit back and do what I please for a while. And I haven't told you the best part. The editor wrote saying how much he liked the yarn and asked me for more of the same kind.

EILEEN. And you've the three others about the same person—just as good, too! Why, you'll sell them all! (She clasps her hands delightedly.)

MURRAY. And I can send them out right away. They're all typed, thanks to you. That's what's brought me luck, I know. I never had a bit by myself. (Then, after a quick glance around to make sure they are alone, he bends down and kisses her.) There! A token of gratitude—even if it is against the rules.

EILEEN (flushing—with timid happiness). Stephen! You mustn't! They'll see.

MURRAY (boldly). Let them!

EILEEN. But you know—they've warned us against being so much together, already.

MURRAY. Let them! We'll be out of this prison soon. (Eileen shakes her head sadly, but he does not notice.) Oh, I wish you could leave when I do. We'd have some celebration together.

EILEEN (her lips trembling). I was thinking last night—that you'd soon be going away. You look so well. Do you think—they'll let you go—soon?

MURRAY. You bet I do. I'm bound to go now. It's ridiculous keeping me here when I'm as healthy as a pig. I caught Stanton in the hall last night and asked him if I could go.

EILEEN (anxiously). What did he say?

MURRAY. He only smiled and said: "We'll see if you gain weight to-morrow." As if that mattered now! Why, I'm way above normal as it is! But you know Stanton—always putting you off. But I could tell by the way he said it he'd be willing to consider——

EILEEN (slowly). Then—if you gain to-day—-

MURRAY. He'll let me go. Yes, I know he will. I'm going to insist on it.

EILEEN. Then—you'll leave——?

MURRAY. Right away. The minute I can get packed.

EILEEN (trying to force a smile). Oh, I'm so glad—for your sake; but—I'm selfish—it'll be so lonely here without you.

MURRAY (consolingly). You'll be going away yourself before long. (Eileen shakes her head. He goes on without noticing, wrapped in his own success.) Oh, Eileen, you can't imagine all it opens up for me—selling that story. I don't have to go back home to stagnate. I can go straight to New York, and live, and meet real people who are doing things. I can take my time, and try and do the work I hope to. (Feelingly.) You don't know how grateful I am to you, Eileen—how you've helped me. Oh, I don't mean just the typing, I mean your encouragement, your faith! I'd never have had guts enough to stick to it myself. The stories would never have been written if it hadn't been for you.

EILEEN (choking back a sob). I didn't do—anything.

MURRAY (staring down at her—with rough kindliness). Here, here, that'll never do! You're not weeping about it, are you, silly? (He pats her on the shoulder.) What's the matter, Eileen? You didn't eat a thing this morning. I was watching you. (With kindly severity.) That's no way to gain weight, you know. You'll have to feed up. Do you hear what your guardian commands, eh?

EILEEN (with dull hopelessness). I know I'll lose again. I've been losing steadily the past three weeks.

MURRAY. Here! Don't you dare talk that way! I won't stand for it. Why, you've been picking up wonderfully—until just lately. You've made such a game fight for four months. Even the old Doc has told you how much he admired your pluck, and how much better you were getting. You're not going to quit now, are you?

EILEEN (despairingly). Oh, I don't care! I don't care—now.

MURRAY. Now? What do you mean by that? What's happened to make things any different?

EILEEN (evasively). Oh—nothing. Don't ask me, Stephen.

MURRAY (with sudden anger). I don't have to ask you. I can guess. Another letter from home—or from that ass, eh?

EILEEN (shaking her head). No, it isn't that. (She looks at him as if imploring him to comprehend.)

MURRAY (furiously). Of course, you'd deny it. You always do. But don't you suppose I've got eyes? It's been the same damn thing all the time you've been here. After every nagging letter—thank God they don't write often any more!—you've been all in; and after their Sunday visits—you can thank God they've been few, too—you're utterly knocked out. It's a shame! The selfish swine!

EILEEN. Stephen!

MURRAY (relentlessly.) Don't be sentimental, Eileen. You know it's true. From what you've told me of their letters, their visits—from what I've seen and suspected—they've done nothing but worry and torment you and do their best to keep you from getting well.

EILEEN (faintly). You're not fair, Stephen.

MURRAY. Rot! When it isn't your father grumbling about expense, it's the kids, or that stupid housekeeper, or that slick Aleck, Nicholls, with his cowardly lies. Which is it this time?

EILEEN (pitifully). None of them.

MURRAY (explosively). But him, especially—the dirty cad! Oh, I've got a rich notion to pay a call on that gentleman when I leave and tell him what I think of him.

EILEEN (quickly). No—you mustn't ever! He's not to blame. If you knew—— (She stops, lowering her eyes in confusion.)

MURRAY (roughly). Knew what? You make me sick, Eileen—always finding excuses for him. I never could understand what a girl like you could see—— But what's the use? I've said all this before. You're wasting yourself on a—— (Rudely.) Love must be blind. And yet you say you don't love him, really?

EILEEN (shaking her head—helplessly). But I do—like Fred. We've been good friends so many years. I don't want to hurt him—his pride——

MURRAY. That's the same as answering no to my question. Then, if you don't love him, why don't you write and tell him to go to—break it off? (Eileen bows her head, but doesn't reply. Irritated, Murray continues brutally.) Are you afraid it would break his heart? Don't be a fool! The only way you could do that would be to deprive him of his meals.

EILEEN (springing to her feet—distractedly). Please stop, Stephen! You're cruel! And you've been so kind—the only real friend I've had up here. Don't spoil it all now.

MURRAY (remorsefully). I'm sorry, Eileen. I was only talking. I won't say another word. (Irritably.) Still, someone ought to say or do something to put a stop to——

EILEEN (with a broken laugh). Never mind. Everything will stop—soon, now!

MURRAY (suspiciously). What do you mean?

EILEEN (with an attempt at a careless tone). Nothing. If you can't see—— (She turns to him with sudden intensity.) Oh, Stephen, if you only knew how wrong you are about everything you've said. It's all true; but it isn't that—any of it—any more—that's—— Oh, I can't tell you!

MURRAY (with great interest). Please do, Eileen!

EILEEN (with a helpless laugh). No.

MURRAY. Please tell me what it is! Let me help you.

EILEEN. No. It wouldn't be any use, Stephen.

MURRAY (offended). Why do you say that? Haven't I helped before?

EILEEN. Yes—but this——

MURRAY. Come now! 'Fess up! What is "this"?

EILEEN. No. I couldn't speak of it here, anyway. They'll all be coming out soon.

MURRAY (insistently). Then when? Where?

EILEEN. Oh, I don't know—perhaps never, nowhere. I don't know—— Sometime before you leave, maybe.

MURRAY. But I may go to-morrow morning—if I gain weight and Stanton lets me.

EILEEN (sadly). Yes, I was forgetting—you were going right away. (Dully). Then nowhere, I suppose—never. (Glancing towards the dining-room.) They're all getting up. Let's not talk about it any more—now.

MURRAY (stubbornly). But you'll tell me later, Eileen? You must.

EILEEN (vaguely). Perhaps. It depends——

(The patients, about forty in number, straggle in from the dining-room by twos and threes, chatting in low tones. The men and women with few exceptions separate into two groups, the women congregating in the left right angle of chairs, the men sitting or standing in the right right angle. In appearance, most of the patients are tanned, healthy, and cheerful-looking. The great majority are under middle age. Their clothes are of the cheap, ready-made variety. They are all distinctly of the wage-earning class. They might well be a crowd of cosmopolitan factory workers gathered together after a summer vacation. A hollow-chestedness and a tendency to round shoulders may be detected as a common characteristic. A general air of tension, marked by frequent bursts of laughter in too high a key, seems to pervade the throng. Murray and Eileen, as if to avoid contact with the others, come over to the right in front of the dining-room door.)

MURRAY (in a low voice). Listen to them laugh. Did you ever notice—perhaps it's my imagination—how forced they act on Saturday mornings before they're weighed?

EILEEN (dully). No.

MURRAY. Can't you tell me that secret now? No one'll hear.

EILEEN (vehemently). No, no, how could I? Don't speak of it!

(A sudden silence falls on all the groups at once. Their eyes, by a common impulse, turn quickly towards the door to the hall.)

A WOMAN (nervously—as if this moment's silent pause oppressed her.) Play something, Peters. They ain't coming yet.

(Peters, a stupid-looking young fellow with a sly, twisted smirk which gives him the appearance of perpetually winking his eye, detaches himself from a group on the right. All join in with urging exclamations: "Go on, Peters! Go to it! Pedal up, Pete! Give us a rag! That's the boy, Peters!" etc.)

PETERS. Sure, if I got time.

(He goes to the pianola and puts in a roll. The mingled conversation and laughter bursts forth again as he sits on the bench and starts pedalling.)

MURRAY (disgustedly). It's sure good to think I won't have to listen to that old tin-pan being banged much longer!

(The music interrupts him—a quick rag. The patients brighten, hum, whistle, sway their heads or tap their feet in time to the tune. Doctor Stanton and Doctor Simms appear in the doorway from the hall. All eyes are turned on them.)

STANTON (raising his voice). They all seem to be here, Doctor. We might as well start.

(Mrs. Turner, the matron, comes in behind them—a stout, motherly, capable-looking woman with grey hair. She hears Stanton's remark.)

MRS. TURNER. And take temperatures after, Doctor?

STANTON. Yes, Mrs. Turner. I think that's better to-day.

MRS. TURNER. All right, Doctor.

(Stanton and the assistant go out. Mrs. Turner advances a step or so into the room and looks from one group of patients to the other, inclining her head and smiling benevolently. All force smiles and nod in recognition of her greeting. Peters, at the pianola, lets the music slow down, glancing questioningly at the matron to see if she is going to order it stopped. Then, encouraged by her smile, his feet pedal harder than ever.)

MURRAY. Look at old Mrs. Grundy's eyes pinned on us! She'll accuse us of being too familiar again, the old wench!

EILEEN. Sssh. You're wrong. She's looking at me, not at us.

MURRAY. At you? Why?

EILEEN. I ran a temperature yesterday. It must have been over a hundred last night.

MURRAY. (with consoling scepticism). You're always looking for trouble, Eileen. How do you know you ran a temp? You didn't see the stick, I suppose?

EILEEN. No—but—I could tell. I felt feverish and chilly. It must have been way up.

MURRAY. Bosh! If it was you'd have been sent to bed.

EILEEN. That's why she's looking at me. (Piteously.) Oh, I do hope I won't be sent back to bed! I don't know what I'd do. If I could only gain this morning. If my temp has only gone down! (Hopelessly.) But I feel—— I didn't sleep a wink—thinking——

MURRAY. (roughly). You'll persuade yourself you've got leprosy in a second. Don't be silly! It's all imagination, I tell you. You'll gain. Wait and see if you don't.

(Eileen shakes her head. A metallic rumble and jangle comes from the hallway. Everyone turns in that direction with nervous expectancy.)

MRS. TURNER (admonishingly). Mr. Peters!

PETERS. Yes, ma'am.

(He stops playing and rejoins the group of men on the right. In the midst of a silence broken only by hushed murmurs of conversation, Doctor Stanton appears in the hall doorway. He turns to help his assistant wheel in a Fairbanks scale on castors. They place the scale against the wall immediately to the rear of the doorway. Doctor Simms adjusts it to a perfect balance.)

DOCTOR STANTON (takes a pencil from his pocket and opens the record book he has in his hand). All ready, Doctor?

DOCTOR SIMMS. Just a second, sir.

(A chorus of coughs comes from the impatient crowd, and handkerchiefs are hurriedly produced to shield mouths.)

MURRAY (with a nervous smile). Well, we're all set. Here's hoping!

EILEEN. You'll gain, I'm sure you will. You look so well.

MURRAY. Oh—I—I wasn't thinking of myself, I'm a sure thing. I was betting on you. I've simply got to gain to-day, when so much depends on it.

EILEEN. Yes, I hope you—— (She falters brokenly and turns away from him.)

DOCTOR SIMMS (straightening up). All ready, Doctor?

STANTON (nods and glances at his book—without raising his voice—distinctly). Mrs. Abner.

(A middle-aged woman comes and gets on the scale. Simms adjusts it to her weight of the previous week, which Stanton reads to him from the book in a low voice, and weighs her.)

MURRAY (with a relieved sigh). They're off. (Noticing Eileen's downcast head and air of dejection.) Here! Buck up, Eileen! Old Lady Grundy's watching you—and it's your turn in a second.

(Eileen raises her head and forces a frightened smile. Mrs. Abner gets down off the scale with a pleased grin. She has evidently gained. She rejoins the group of women, chattering volubly in low tones. Her exultant "gained half a pound" can be heard. The other women smile their perfunctory congratulations, their eyes absent-minded, intent on their own worries. Stanton writes down the weight in the book.)

STANTON. Miss Bailey. (A young girl goes to the scales.)

MURRAY. Bailey looks bad, doesn't she?

EILEEN (her lips trembling). She's been losing, too.

MURRAY. Well, you're going to gain to-day. Remember, now!

EILEEN (with a feeble smile). I'll try to obey your orders.

(Miss Bailey goes down off the scales. Her eyes are full of despondency although she tries to make a brave face of it, forcing a laugh as she joins the women. They stare at her with pitying looks and murmur consoling phrases.)

EILEEN. She's lost again. Oh, I wish I didn't have to get weighed——

STANTON. Miss Carmody.

(Eileen starts nervously.)

MURRAY (as she leaves him). Remember now! Break the scales!

(She walks quickly to the scales, trying to assume an air of defiant indifference. The balance stays down as she steps up. Eileen's face shows her despair at this. Simms weighs her and gives the poundage in a low voice to Stanton. Eileen steps down mechanically, then hesitates as if not knowing where to turn, her anguished eyes flitting from one group to another.)

MURRAY (savagely). Damn!

(Doctor Stanton writes the figures in his book, glances sharply at Eileen, and then nods significantly to Mrs. Turner who is standing beside him.)

STANTON (calling the next). Miss Doeffler.

(Another woman comes to be weighed.)

MRS. TURNER. Miss Carmody! Will you come here a moment, please?

EILEEN (her face growing very pale). Yes, Mrs. Turner.

(The heads of the different groups bend together. Their eyes follow Eileen as they whisper. Mrs. Turner leads her down front, left. Behind them the weighing of the women continues briskly. The great majority have gained. Those who have not have either remained stationary or lost a negligible fraction of a pound. So, as the weighing proceeds, the general air of smiling satisfaction rises among the groups of women. Some of them, their ordeal over, go out through the hall doorway by twos and threes with suppressed laughter and chatter. As they pass behind Eileen they glance at her with pitying curiosity. Doctor Stanton's voice is heard at regular intervals calling the names in alphabetical order: Mrs. Elbing, Miss Finch, Miss Grimes, Miss Haines, Miss Hayes, Miss Jutner, Miss Linowski, Mrs. Marini, Mrs. McCoy, Miss McElroy, Miss Nelson, Mrs. Nott, Mrs. O'Brien, Mrs. Olson, Miss Paul, Miss Petrovski, Mrs. Quinn, Miss Robersi, Mrs. Stattler, Miss Unger.)

MRS. TURNER (putting her hand on Eileen's shoulder—kindly). You're not looking so well lately, my dear, do you know it?

EILEEN (bravely). I feel—fine. (Her eyes, as if looking for encouragement, seek Murray, who is staring at her worriedly.)

MRS. TURNER (gently). You lost weight again, you know.

EILEEN, I know—but——

MRS. TURNER. This is the fourth week.

EILEEN. I—I know it is——

MRS. TURNER. I've been keeping my eye on you. You seem—worried. Are you upset about—something we don't know?

EILEEN (quickly). No, no! I haven't slept much lately. That must be it.

MRS. TURNER. Are you worrying about your condition? Is that what keeps you awake?

EILEEN. No.

MRS. TURNER. You're sure it's not that?

EILEEN. Yes, I'm sure it's not, Mrs. Turner.

MRS. TURNER. I was going to tell you if you were: Don't do it! You can't expect it to be all smooth sailing. Even the most favourable cases have to expect these little setbacks. A few days' rest in bed will start you on the right trail again.

EILEEN (in anguish, although she had realised this was coming). Bed? Go back to bed? Oh, Mrs. Turner!

MRS. TURNER (gently). Yes, my dear, Doctor Stanton thinks it best. So when you go back to your cottage——

EILEEN. Oh, please—not to-day—not right away!

MRS. TURNER. You had a temperature and a high pulse yesterday, didn't you realise it? And this morning you look quite feverish. (She tries to put her hand on Eileen's forehead, but the latter steps away defensively.)

EILEEN. It's only—not sleeping last night. I was nervous. Oh, I'm sure it'll go away.

MRS. TURNER (consolingly). When you lie still and have perfect rest, of course it will.

EILEEN (with a longing look over at Murray). But not to-day—please, Mrs. Turner.

MRS. TURNER (looking at her keenly). There is something upsetting you. You've something on your mind that you can't tell me, is that it? (Eileen maintains a stubborn silence.) But think—can't you tell me? (With a kindly smile.) I'm used to other people's troubles. I've been playing mother-confessor to the patients for years now, and I think I've usually been able to help them. Can't you confide in me, child? (Eileen drops her eyes, but remains silent. Mrs. Turner glances meaningly over at Murray, who is watching them whenever he thinks the matron is not aware of it—a note of sharp rebuke in her voice.) I think I can guess your secret, my dear, even if you're too stubborn to tell. This setback is your own fault. You've let other notions become more important to you than the idea of getting well. And you've no excuse for it. After I had to warn you a month ago, I expected that silliness to stop instantly.

EILEEN (her face flushed—protesting). There never was anything. Nothing like that has anything to do with it.

MRS. TURNER (sceptically). What is it that has, then?

EILEEN (lying determinedly). It's my family. They keep writing—and worrying me—and—— That's what it is, Mrs. Turner.

MRS. TURNER (not exactly knowing whether to believe this or not—probing the girl with her eyes). Your father?

EILEEN. Yes, all of them. (Suddenly seeing a way to discredit all of the matron's suspicions—excitedly.) And principally the young man I'm engaged to—the one who came to visit me several times——

MRS. TURNER (surprised). So—you're engaged? (Eileen nods. Mrs. Turner immediately dismisses her suspicions.) Oh, pardon me. I didn't know that, you see, or I wouldn't—— (She pats Eileen on the shoulder comfortingly.) Never mind. You'll tell me all about it, won't you?

EILEEN (desperately). Yes. (She seems about to go on, but the matron interrupts her.)

MRS. TURNER. Oh, not here, my dear. Now now. Come to my room—let me see—I'll be busy all the morning—some time this afternoon. Will you do that?

EILEEN. Yes. (Joyfully.) Then I needn't go to bed right away?

MRS. TURNER. No—on one condition. You mustn't take any exercise. Stay in your recliner all day and rest and remain in bed to-morrow morning. And promise me you will rest and not worry any more about things we can easily fix up between us.

EILEEN. I promise, Mrs. Turner.

MRS. TURNER (smiling in dismissal). Very well, then. I must speak to Miss Bailey. I'll see you this afternoon.

EILEEN. Yes, Mrs. Turner.

(The matron goes to the rear where Miss Bailey is sitting with Mrs. Abner. She beckons to Miss Bailey, who gets up with a scared look, and they go to the far left corner of the room. Eileen stands for a moment hesitating—then starts to go to Murray, but just at this moment Peters comes forward and speaks to Murray.)

PETERS (with his sly twisted grin). Say, Carmody musta lost fierce. Did yuh see the Old Woman handin' her an earful? Sent her back to bed, I betcha. What d'yuh think?

MURRAY (impatiently, showing his dislike). How the hell do I know?

PETERS (sneeringly). Huh, you don't know nothin' 'bout her, I s'pose? Where d'yuh get that stuff? Think yuh're kiddin' me?

MURRAY (with cold rage before which the other slinks away). Peters, the more I see of you the better I like a skunk! If it wasn't for other people losing weight you couldn't get any joy out of life, could you? (Roughly.) Get away from me! (He makes a threatening gesture.)

PETERS (beating a snarling retreat). Wait 'n' see if yuh don't lose too, yuh stuck-up boob!

(Seeing that Murray is alone again, Eileen starts towards him, but this time she is intercepted by Mrs. Abner, who stops on her way out. The weighing of the women is now finished, and that of the men, which proceeds much quicker, begins.)

STANTON. Anderson!

(Anderson comes to the scales. The men all move down to the left to wait their turn, with the exception of Murray, who remains by the dining-room door, fidgeting impatiently, anxious for a word with Eileen.)

MRS. ABNER (taking Eileen's arm). Coming over to the cottage, dearie?

EILEEN. Not just this minute, Mrs. Abner. I have to wait——

MRS. ABNER. For the Old Woman? You lost to-day, didn't you? Is she sendin' you to bed, the old devil?

EILEEN. Yes, I'm afraid I'll have to——

MRS. ABNER. She's a mean one, ain't she? I gained this week—half a pound. Lord, I'm gittin' fat! All my clothes are gittin' too small for me. Don't know what I'll do. Did you lose much, dearie?

EILEEN. Three pounds.

MRS. ABNER. Ain't that awful! (Hastening to make up for this thoughtless remark.) All the same, what's three pounds! You can git them back in a week after you're resting more. You been runnin' a temp, too, ain't you? (Eileen nods.) Don't worry about it, dearie. It'll go down. Worryin's the worst. Me, I don't never worry none. (She chuckled with satisfaction—then soberly.) I just been talkin' with Bailey. She's got to go to bed, too, I guess. She lost two pounds. She ain't runnin' no temp though.

STANTON. Barnes! (Another man comes to the scales.)

MRS. ABNER (in a mysterious whisper). Look at Mr. Murray, dearie. Ain't he nervous to-day? I don't know as I blame him, either. I heard the doctor said he'd let him go home if he gained to-day. Is it true, d'you know?

EILEEN (dully). I don't know.

MRS. ABNER. Gosh, I wish it was me! My old man's missin' me like the dickens, he writes. (She starts to go.) You'll be over to the cottage in a while, won't you? Me 'n' you'll have a game of casino, eh?

EILEEN (happy at this deliverance). Yes, I'll be glad to.

STANTON. Cordero!

(Mrs. Abner goes out. Eileen again starts towards Murray, but this time Flynn, a young fellow with a brick-coloured, homely, good-natured face, and a shaven-necked haircut, slouches back to Murray. Eileen is brought to a halt in front of the table where she stands, her face working with nervous strain, clasping and unclasping her trembling hands.)

FLYNN (curiously). Say, Steve, what's this bull about the Doc lettin' yuh beat it if yuh gain to-day? Is it straight goods?

MURRAY. He said he might, that's all. (Impatiently.) How the devil did that story get travelling around?

FLYNN (with a grin). Wha' d'yuh expect with this gang of skirts chewin' the fat? Well, here's hopin' yuh come home a winner, Steve.

MURRAY (gratefully). Thanks. (With confidence.) Oh, I'll gain all right; but whether he'll let me go or not—— (He shrugs his shoulders.)

FLYNN. Make 'em believe. I wish Stanton'd ask waivers on me. (With a laugh.) I oughter gain a ton to-day. I ate enough spuds for breakfast to plant a farm.

STANTON. Flynn!

FLYNN. Me to the plate! (He strides to the scales.)

MURRAY. Good luck!

(He starts to join Eileen, but Miss Bailey, who has finished her talk with Mrs. Turner, who goes out to the hall, approaches Eileen at just this moment. Murray stops in his tracks, fuming. He and Eileen exchange a glance of helpless annoyance.)

MISS BAILEY (her thin face full of the satisfaction of misery finding company—plucks at Eileen's sleeve). Say, Carmody, she sent you back to bed, too, didn't she?

EILEEN (absent-mindedly). I suppose——

MISS BAILEY. You suppose? Don't you know? Of course she did. I got to go, too. (Pulling Eileen's sleeve.) Come on. Let's get out of here. I hate this place, don't you?

STANTON (calling the next). Hopper!

FLYNN (shouts to Murray as he is going out to the hall). I hit 'er for a two-bagger, Steve. Come on now, Bo, and bring me home! 'Atta, boy! (Grinning gleefully, he slouches out. Doctor Stanton and all the patients laugh.)

MISS BAILEY (with irritating persistence). Come on, Carmody. You've got to go to bed, too.

EILEEN (at the end of her patience—releasing her arm from the other's grasp). Let me alone, will you? I don't have to go to bed now—not till to-morrow morning.

MISS BAILEY (despairingly, as if she couldn't believe her ears). You don't have to go to bed?

EILEEN. Not now—no.

MISS BAILEY (in a whining rage). Why not? You've been running a temp, too, and I haven't. You must have a pull, that's what! It isn't fair. I'll bet you lost more than I did, too! What right have you got—— Well, I'm not going to bed if you don't. Wait 'n' see!

EILEEN (turning away, revolted). Go away! Leave me alone, please.

STANTON. Lowenstein!

MISS BAILEY (turns to the hall door, whining). All right for you! I'm going to find out. It isn't square. I'll write home.

(She disappears in the hallway. Murray strides over to Eileen, whose strength seems to have left her and who is leaning weakly against the table.)

MURRAY. Thank God—at last! Isn't it hell—all these fools! I couldn't get to you. What did Old Lady Grundy have to say to you? I saw her giving me a hard look. Was it about us—the old stuff? (Eileen nods with downcast eyes.) What did she say? Never mind now. You can tell me in a minute. It's my turn next. (His eyes glance towards the scales.)

EILEEN (intensely). Oh, Stephen, I wish you weren't going away!

MURRAY (excitedly). Maybe I'm not. It's exciting—like gambling—if I win——

STANTON. Murray!

MURRAY. Wait here, Eileen.

(He goes to the scales. Eileen keeps her back turned. Her body stiffens rigidly in the intensity of her conflicting emotions. She stares straight ahead, her eyes full of anguish. Murray steps on the scales nervously. The balance rod hits the top smartly. He has gained. His face lights up and he heaves a great sigh of relief. Eileen seems to sense this outcome and her head sinks, her body sags weakly and seems to shrink to a smaller size. Murray gets off the scales, his face beaming with a triumphant smile. Doctor Stanton smiles and murmurs something to him in a low voice. Murray nods brightly; then turns back to Eileen.)

STANTON. Nathan! (Another patient advances to the scales.)

MURRAY (trying to appear casual). Well—three rousing cheers! Stanton told me to come to his office at eleven. That means a final exam—and release!

EILEEN (dully). So you gained?

MURRAY. Three pounds.

EILEEN. Funny—I lost three. (With a pitiful effort at a smile.) I hope you gained the ones I lost. (Her lips tremble.) So you're surely going away.

MURRAY (his joy fleeing as he is confronted with her sorrow—slowly). It looks that way, Eileen.

EILEEN (in a trembling whisper broken by rising sobs). Oh—I'm so glad—you gained—the ones I lost, Stephen—— So glad! (She breaks down, covering her face with her hands, stifling her sobs.)

MURRAY (alarmed). Eileen! What's the matter? (Desperately.) Stop it! Stanton'll see you!

THE CURTAIN FALLS

ACT TWO: SCENE TWO

Midnight of the same day. A cross-road near the sanatorium. The main road comes down forward from the right. A smaller road, leading down from the left, joins it towards left centre.

Dense woods rise sheer from the grass and bramble-grown ditches at the roadsides. At the junction of the two roads there is a signpost, its arms pointing towards the right and the left, rear. A pile of round stones is at the road corner, left forward. A full moon, riding high overhead, throws the roads into white, shadowless relief and masses the woods into walls of compact blackness. The trees lean heavily together, their branches motionless, unstirred by any trace of wind.

As the curtain rises, Eileen is discovered standing in the middle of the road, front centre. Her face shows white and clear in the bright moonlight as she stares with anxious expectancy up the road to the left. Her body is fixed in an attitude of rigid immobility as if she were afraid the slightest movement would break the spell of silence and awaken the unknown. She has shrunk instinctively as far away as she can from the mysterious darkness which rises at the roadsides like an imprisoning wall. A sound of hurried footfalls, muffled by the dust, comes from the road she is watching. She gives a startled gasp. Her eyes strain to identify the oncomer. Uncertain, trembling with fright, she hesitates a second; then darts to the side of the road and crouches down in the shadow.

Stephen Murray comes down the road from the left. He stops by the signpost and peers about him. He wears a cap, the peak of which casts his face into shadow. Finally he calls in a low voice.

MURRAY. Eileen!

EILEEN (coming out quickly from her hiding-place—with a glad little cry). Stephen! At last! (She runs to him as if she were going to fling her arms about him, but stops abashed. He reaches out and takes her hands.)

MURRAY. At last? It can't be twelve yet. (He leads her to the pile of stones on the left.) I haven't heard the village clock.

EILEEN. I must have come early. It seemed as if I'd been waiting for ages. I was so anxious——

MURRAY. How your hands tremble! Were you frightened?

EILEEN (forcing a smile). A little. The woods are so black—and queer-looking. I'm all right now.

MURRAY. Sit down. You must rest. (In a tone of annoyed reproof.) I'm going to read you a lecture, young lady. You shouldn't ever have done this—running a temp and—— Good heavens, don't you want to get well?

EILEEN (dully). I don't know——

MURRAY (irritably). You make me ill when you talk that way, Eileen. It doesn't sound like you at all. What's come over you lately? Get a grip on yourself, for God's sake. I was—knocked out—when I read the note you slipped me after supper. I didn't get a chance to read it until late, I was so busy packing, and by that time you'd gone to your cottage. If I could have reached you any way I'd have refused to come here, I tell you straight. But I couldn't—and I knew you'd be here waiting—and—still, I feel guilty. Damn it, this isn't the thing for you! You ought to be in bed asleep. Can't you look out for yourself?

EILEEN (humbly). Please, Stephen, don't scold me.

MURRAY. How the devil did you ever get the idea—meeting me here at this ungodly hour?

EILEEN. You'd told me about your sneaking out that night to go to the village, and I thought there'd be no harm this one night—the last night.

MURRAY. But I'm well. I've been well. It's different. You—— Honest, Eileen, you shouldn't lose sleep and tax your strength.

EILEEN. Don't scold me, please. I'll make up for it. I'll rest all the time—after you're gone. I just had to see you some way—somewhere where there weren't eyes and ears on all sides—when you told me after dinner that Doctor Stanton had examined you and said you could go to-morrow—— (A clock in the distant village begins striking.) Sssh! Listen.

MURRAY. That's twelve now. You see I was early.

(In a pause of silence they wait motionlessly until the last mournful note dies in the hushed woods.)

EILEEN (in a stifled voice). It isn't to-morrow now, is it? It's to-day—the day you're going.

MURRAY (something in her voice making him avert his face and kick at the heap of stones on which she is sitting—brusquely). Well, I hope you took precautions so you wouldn't be caught sneaking out.

EILEEN. I did just what you'd told me you did—stuffed the pillows under the clothes so the watchman would think I was there.

MURRAY. None of the patients on your porch saw you leave, did they?

EILEEN. No. They were all asleep.

MURRAY. That's all right, then. I wouldn't trust any of that bunch of women. They'd be only too glad to squeal on you. (There is an uncomfortable pause. Murray seems waiting for her to speak. He looks about him at the trees, up into the moonlit sky, breathing in the fresh air with a healthy delight. Eileen remains with downcast head, staring at the road.) It's beautiful to-night, isn't it? Worth losing sleep for.

EILEEN (dully). Yes. (Another pause—finally she murmurs faintly.) Are you leaving early?

MURRAY. The ten-forty. Leave the San at ten, I guess.

EILEEN. You're going home?

MURRAY. Home? You mean to the town? No. But I'm going to see my sisters—just to say hello. I've got to, I suppose. I won't stay more than a few days, if I can help it.

EILEEN. I'm sure—I've often felt—you're unjust to your sisters. (With conviction.) I'm sure they must both love you.

MURRAY (frowning). Maybe, in their own way. But what's love without a glimmer of understanding—a nuisance! They have never seen the real me and never have wanted to—that's all.

EILEEN (as if to herself). What is—the real you? (Murray kicks at the stones impatiently without answering. Eileen hastens to change the subject.) And then you'll go to New York?

MURRAY (interested, at once). Yes. You bet.

EILEEN. And write more?

MURRAY. Not in New York, no. I'm going there to take a vacation, and live, really enjoy myself for a while. I've enough money for that as it is, and if the other stories you typed sell—I'll be as rich as Rockefeller. I might even travel—— No, I've got to make good with my best stuff first. I'll save the travelling as a reward, a prize to gain. That'll keep me at it. I know what I'll do. When I've had enough of New York, I'll rent a place in the country—some old farmhouse—and live alone there and work. (Lost in his own plans—with pleasure.) That's the right idea, isn't it?

EILEEN (trying to appear enthused). It ought to be fine for your work. (After a pause.) They're fine, those stories you wrote here. They're—so much like you. I'd know it was you wrote them even if—I didn't know.

MURRAY (pleased). Wait till you read the others I'm going to do! (After a slight pause—with a good-natured grin.) Here I am talking about myself again! Why don't you call me down when I start that drivel? But you don't know how good it is to have your dreams coming true. It'd make an egotist out of anyone.

EILEEN (sadly). No. I don't know. But I love to hear you talk of yours.

MURRAY (with an embarrassed laugh). Thanks. Well, I've certainly told you all of them. You're the only one—— (He stops and abruptly changes the subject.) You said in your note that you had something important to tell me. (He sits down beside her, crossing his legs.) Is it about your interview with Old Mrs. Grundy this afternoon?

EILEEN. No, that didn't amount to anything. She seemed mad because I told her so little. I think she guessed I only told her what I did so she'd let me stay up, maybe—your last day,—and to keep her from thinking what she did—about us.

MURRAY (quickly, as if he wishes to avoid this subject). What is it you wanted to tell me, then?

EILEEN (sadly). It doesn't seem so important now, somehow. I suppose it was silly of me to drag you out here, just for that. It can't mean anything to you—much.

MURRAY (encouragingly). How do you know it can't?

EILEEN (slowly). I only thought—you might like to know.

MURRAY (interestedly). Know what? What is it? If I can help——

EILEEN. No. (After a moment's hesitation.) I wrote to him this afternoon.

MURRAY. Him?

EILEEN. The letter you've been advising me to write.

MURRAY (as if the knowledge of this alarmed him—haltingly). You mean—Fred Nicholls?

EILEEN. Yes.

MURRAY (after a pause—uncomfortably). You mean—you broke it all off?

EILEEN. Yes—for good. (She looks up at his averted face. He remains silent. She continues apprehensively.) You don't say anything. I thought—you'd be glad. You've always told me it was the honourable thing to do.

MURRAY (gruffly). I know. I say more than my prayers, damn it! (With sudden eagerness.) Have you mailed the letter yet?

EILEEN. Yes. Why?

MURRAY (shortly). Humph. Oh—nothing.

EILEEN (with pained disappointment). Oh, Stephen, you don't think I did wrong, do you—now—after all you've said?

MURRAY (hurriedly). Wrong? No, not if you were convinced it was the right thing to do yourself—if you know you don't love him. But I'd hate to think you did it just on my advice. I shouldn't—— I didn't mean to interfere. I don't know enough about your relations for my opinion to count.

EILEEN (hurt). You know all there is to know.

MURRAY. I didn't mean—anything like that. I know you've been frank. But him—I don't know him. How could I, just meeting him once? He may be quite different from my idea. That's what I'm getting at. I don't want to be unfair to him.

EILEEN (bitterly scornful). You needn't worry. You weren't unfair. And you needn't be afraid you were responsible for my writing. I'd been going to for a long time before you ever spoke.

MURRAY (with a relieved sigh). I'm glad of that—honestly, Eileen. I felt guilty. I shouldn't have knocked him behind his back without knowing him at all.

EILEEN. You said you could read him like a book from his letters I showed you.

MURRAY (apologetically). I know. I'm a fool.

EILEEN (angrily). What makes you so considerate of Fred Nicholls all of a sudden? What you thought about him was right.

MURRAY (vaguely). I don't know. One makes mistakes.

EILEEN (assertively). Well, I know! You needn't waste pity on him. He'll be only too glad to get my letter. He's been anxious to be free of me ever since I was sent here, only he thought it wouldn't be decent to break it off himself while I was sick. He was afraid of what people would say about him when they found it out. So he's just gradually stopped writing and coming for visits, and waited for me to realise. And if I didn't, I know he'd have broken it off himself the first day I got home. I've kept persuading myself that, in spite of the way he's acted, he did love me as much as he could love anyone, and that it would hurt him if I—— But now I know that he never loved me, that he couldn't love anyone but himself. Oh, I don't hate him for it. He can't help being what he is. And all people seem to be—like that, mostly. I'm only going to remember that he and I grew up together, and that he was kind to me then when he thought he liked me—and forget all the rest. (With agitated impatience.) Oh, Stephen, you know all this I've said about him. Why don't you admit it? You've read his letters.

MURRAY (haltingly). Yes, I'll admit that was my opinion—only I wanted to be sure you'd found out for yourself.

EILEEN (defiantly). Well, I have! You see that now, don't you?

MURRAY. Yes; and I'm glad you're free of him, for your own sake. I knew he wasn't the person. (With an attempt at a joking tone.) You must get one of the right sort—next time.

EILEEN (springing to her feet with a cry of pain). Stephen!

(He avoids her eyes, which search his face pleadingly.)

MURRAY (mumbling). He wasn't good enough—to lace your shoes—nor anyone else, either.

EILEEN (with a nervous laugh). Don't be silly. (After a pause, during which she waits hungrily for some word from him—with a sigh of despair—faintly.) Well, I've told you—all there is. I might as well go back.

MURRAY (not looking at her—indistinctly). Yes. You mustn't lose too much sleep. I'll come to your cottage in the morning to say good-bye. They'll permit that, I guess.

EILEEN (stands looking at him imploringly, her face convulsed with anguish, but he keeps his eyes fixed on the rocks at his feet. Finally she seems to give up and takes a few uncertain steps up the road towards the right—in an exhausted whisper). Good night, Stephen.

MURRAY (his voice choked and husky). Good night, Eileen.

EILEEN (walks weakly up the road, but, as she passes the signpost, she suddenly stops and turns to look again at Murray, who has not moved or lifted his eyes. A great shuddering sob shatters her pent-up emotions. She runs back to Murray, her arms outstretched, with a choking cry). Stephen!

MURRAY (startled, whirls to face her and finds her arms thrown around his neck—in a terrified tone). Eileen!

EILEEN (brokenly). I love you, Stephen—you! That's what I wanted to tell!

(She gazes up into his eyes, her face transfigured by the joy and pain of this abject confession.)

MURRAY (wincing as if this were the thing he had feared to hear). Eileen!

EILEEN (pulling down his head with fierce strength and kissing him passionately on the lips). I love you! I will say it! There! (With sudden horror.) Oh, I know I shouldn't kiss you! I mustn't! You're all well—and I——

MURRAY (protesting frenziedly). Eileen! Damn it! Don't say that! What do you think I am!

(He kisses her fiercely two or three times until she forces a hand over her mouth.)

EILEEN (with a hysterically happy laugh). No! Just hold me in your arms—just a little while—before——

MURRAY (his voice trembling). Eileen! Don't talk that way! You're—it's killing me. I can't stand it!

EILEEN (with soothing tenderness). Listen, dear—listen—and you won't say a word—I've so much to say—till I get through—please, will you promise?

MURRAY (between clinched teeth). Yes—anything, Eileen!

EILEEN. Then I want to say—I know your secret. You don't love me—Isn't that it? (Murray groans.) Sssh! It's all right, dear. You can't help what you don't feel. I've guessed you didn't—right along. And I've loved you—such a long time now—always, it seems. And you've sort of guessed—that I did—didn't you? No, don't speak! I'm sure you've guessed—only you didn't want to know—that—did you?—when you didn't love me. That's why you were lying—but I saw, I knew! Oh, I'm not blaming you, darling. How could I—never! You mustn't look so—so frightened. I know how you felt, dear. I've—I've watched you. It was just a flirtation for you at first. Wasn't it? Oh, I know. It was just fun, and—— Please don't look at me so. I'm not hurting you, am I? I wouldn't for worlds, dear—you know—hurt you! And then afterwards—you found we could be such good friends—helping each other—and you wanted it to stay just like that always, didn't you?—I know—and then I had to spoil it all—and fall in love with you—didn't I? Oh, it was stupid—I shouldn't—I couldn't help it, you were so kind and—and different—and I wanted to share in your work and—and everything. I knew you wouldn't want to know I loved you—when you didn't—and I tried hard to be fair and hide my love so you wouldn't see—and I did, didn't I, dear? You never knew till just lately—maybe not till just to-day—did you?—when I knew you were going away so soon—and couldn't help showing it. You never knew before, did you? Did you?

MURRAY (miserably). No. Oh, Eileen—Eileen, I'm so sorry!

EILEEN (in heart-broken protest). Sorry? Oh, no, Stephen, you mustn't be! It's been beautiful—all of it—for me! That's what makes your going—so hard. I had to see you to-night—I'd have gone—crazy—if I didn't know you knew, if I hadn't made you guess. And I thought—if you knew about my writing to Fred—that—maybe—it'd make some difference. (Murray groans—and she laughs hysterically.) I must have been crazy—to think that—mustn't I? As if that could—when you don't love me. Sshh! Please! Let me finish. You mustn't feel sad—or anything. It's made me happier than I've ever been—loving you—even when I did know—you didn't. Only now—you'll forgive me telling you all this, won't you, dear? Now, it's so terrible to think I won't see you any more. I'll feel so—without anybody.

MURRAY (brokenly). But I'll—come back. And you'll be out soon—and then——

EILEEN (brokenly). Sshh! Let me finish. You don't know how alone I am now. Father—he'll marry that housekeeper—and the children—they've forgotten me. None of them need me any more. They've found out how to get on without me—and I'm a drag—dead to them—no place for me home any more—and they'll be afraid to have me back—afraid of catching—I know she won't want me back. And Fred—he's gone—he never mattered, anyway. Forgive me, dear—worrying you—only I want you to know how much you've meant to me—so you won't forget—ever—after you've gone.

MURRAY (in grief-stricken tones). Forget? Eileen! I'll do anything in God's world——

EILEEN. I know—you like me a lot even if you can't love me—don't you? (His arms tighten about her as he bends down and forces a kiss on her lips again.) Oh, Stephen! That was for good-bye. You mustn't come to-morrow morning. I couldn't bear having you—with people watching. But you'll write after—often—won't you? (Heart-brokenly.) Oh, please do that, Stephen!

MURRAY. I will! I swear! And when you get out I'll—we'll—I'll find something. (He kisses her again.)

EILEEN (breaking away from him with a quick movement and stepping back a few feet). Good-bye, darling. Remember me—and perhaps—you'll find out after a time—I'll pray God to make it so! Oh, what am I saying? Only—I'll hope—I'll hope—till I die!

MURRAY (in anguish). Eileen!

EILEEN (her breath coming in tremulous heaves of her bosom). Remember, Stephen—if ever you want—I'll do anything—anything you want—no matter what—I don't care—there's just you and—don't hate me, dear. I love you—love you—remember! (She suddenly turns and runs away up the road.)

MURRAY. Eileen! (He starts to run after her, but stops by the signpost and stamps on the ground furiously, his fists clenched in impotent rage at himself and at fate. He curses hoarsely.) Christ!

THE CURTAIN FALLS

ACT THREE

Four months later. An isolation room at the Infirmary with a sleeping porch at the right of it. Late afternoon of a Sunday towards the end of October. The room, extending two-thirds of the distance from left to right, is, for reasons of space economy, scantily furnished with the bare necessities—a bureau with mirror in the left corner, rear—two straight-backed chairs—a table with a glass top in the centre. The floor is varnished hardwood. The walls and furniture are painted white. On the left, forward, a door to the hall. On the right, rear, a double glass door opening on the porch. Farther front two windows. The porch, a screened-in continuation of the room, contains only a single iron bed, painted white, and a small table placed beside the bed.

The woods, the leaves of the trees rich in their autumn colouring, rise close about this side of the Infirmary. Their branches almost touch the porch on the right. In the rear of the porch they have been cleared away from the building for a narrow space, and through this opening the distant hills can be seen with the tree tops glowing in the sunlight.

As the curtain rises, Eileen is discovered lying in the bed on the porch, propped up into a half-sitting position by pillows under her back and head. She seems to have grown much thinner. Her face is pale and drawn, with deep hollows under her cheek-bones. Her eyes are dull and lustreless. She gazes straight before her into the wood with the unseeing stare of apathetic indifference. The door from the hall in the room behind her is opened, and Miss Howard enters, followed by Bill Carmody, Mrs. Brennan, and Mary. Carmody's manner is unwontedly sober and subdued. This air of respectable sobriety is further enhanced by a black suit, glaringly new and stiffly pressed, a new black derby hat, and shoes polished like a mirror. His expression is full of a bitter, if suppressed, resentment. His gentility is evidently forced upon him in spite of himself and correspondingly irksome. Mrs. Brennan is a tall, stout woman of fifty, lusty and loud-voiced, with a broad, snub-nosed, florid face, a large mouth, the upper lip darkened by a suggestion of moustache, and little round blue eyes, hard and restless with a continual fuming irritation. She is got up regardless in her ridiculous Sunday-best. Mary appears tall and skinny-legged in a starched, outgrown frock. The sweetness of her face has disappeared, giving way to a hang-dog sullenness, a stubborn silence, with sulky, furtive glances of rebellion directed at her step-mother.

MISS HOWARD (pointing to the porch). She's out there on the porch.

MRS. BRENNAN (with dignity). Thank you, ma'am.

MISS HOWARD (with a searching glance at the visitors as if to appraise their intentions). Eileen's been very sick lately, you know, so be careful not to worry her about anything. Do your best to cheer her up.

CARMODY (mournfully). We'll try to put life in her spirits, God help her. (With an uncertain look at Mrs. Brennan.) Won't we, Maggie?

MRS. BRENNAN (turning sharply on Mary, who has gone over to examine the things on the bureau). Come away from that, Mary. Curiosity killed a cat. Don't be touchin' her things. Remember what I told you. Or is it admirin' your mug in the mirror you are? (Turning to Miss Howard as Mary moves away from the bureau, hanging her head—shortly.) Don't you worry, ma'am. We won't trouble Eileen at all.

MISS HOWARD. Another thing. You mustn't say anything to her of what Miss Gilpin just told you about her being sent away to the State Farm in a few days. Eileen isn't to know till the very last minute. It would only disturb her.

CARMODY (hastily). We'll not say a word of it.

MISS HOWARD (turning to the hall door). Thank you.

(She goes out, shutting the door.)

MRS. BRENNAN (angrily). She has a lot of impudent gab, that one, with her don't do this and don't do that! It's a wonder you wouldn't speak up to her and shut her mouth, you great fool, and you payin' money to give her her job. (Disgustedly.) You've no guts in you.

CARMODY (placatingly). Would you have me raisin' a shindy when Eileen's leavin' here in a day or more? What'd be the use?

MRS. BRENNAN. In the new place she's goin' you'll not have to pay a cent, and that's a blessing! It's small good they've done her here for all the money they've taken. (Gazing about the room critically.) It's neat and clean enough; and why shouldn't it, a tiny room and the lot of them nothing to do all day but scrub. (Scornfully.) Two sticks of chairs and a table! They don't give much for the money.

CARMODY. Catch them! It's a good thing she's clearin' out of this, and her worse off after them curin' her eight months than she was when she came. She'll maybe get well in the new place.

MRS. BRENNAN (indifferently). It's God's will, what'll happen. (Irritably.) And I'm thinkin' it's His punishment she's under now for having no heart in her and never writin' home a word to you or the children in two months or more. If the doctor hadn't wrote us himself to come see her, she was sick, we'd have been no wiser.

CARMODY. Whisht! Don't be blamin' a sick girl.

MARY (who has drifted to one of the windows at right—curiously). There's somebody in bed out there. I can't see her face. Is it Eileen?

MRS. BRENNAN. Don't be goin' out there till I tell you, you imp! I must speak to your father first. (Coming closer to him and lowering her voice.) Are you going to tell her about it?

CARMODY (pretending ignorance). About what?

MRS. BRENNAN. About what, indeed! Don't pretend you don't know. About our marryin' two weeks back, of course. What else?

CARMODY (uncertainly). Yes—I disremembered she didn't know. I'll have to tell her, surely.

MRS. BRENNAN (flaring up). You speak like you wouldn't. Is it shamed of me you are? Are you afraid of a slip of a girl? Well, then, I'm not! I'll tell her to her face soon enough.

CARMODY (angry in his turn—assertively). You'll not, now! Keep your mouth out of this and your rough tongue! I tell you I'll tell her.

MRS. BRENNAN (satisfied). Let's be going out to her, then. (They move towards the door to the porch.) And keep your eye on your watch. We mustn't miss the train. Come with us, Mary, and remember to keep your mouth shut.

(They go out on the porch and stand just outside the door waiting for Eileen to notice them; but the girl in bed continues to stare into the woods, oblivious to their presence.)

MRS. BRENNAN (nudging Carmody with her elbow—in a harsh whisper). She don't see us. It's a dream she's in with her eyes open. Glory be, it's bad she's lookin'. The look on her face'd frighten you. Speak to her, you!

(Eileen stirs uneasily as if this whisper had disturbed her unconsciously.)

CARMODY (wetting his lips and clearing his throat huskily). Eileen.

EILEEN (startled, turns and stares at them with frightened eyes. After a pause she ventures uncertainly, as if she were not sure hut what these figures might be creatures of her dream). Father. (Her eyes shift to Mrs. Brennan's face and she shudders.) Mrs. Brennan.

MRS. BRENNAN (quickly—in a voice meant to be kindly). Here we are, all of us, come to see you. How is it you're feelin' now, Eileen?

(While she is talking she advances to the bedside, followed by Carmody, and takes one of the sick girl's hands in hers. Eileen withdraws it as if stung and holds it out to her father. Mrs. Brennan's face flushes angrily and she draws back from the bedside.)

CARMODY (moved—with rough tenderness patting her hand). Ah, Eileen, sure it's a sight for sore eyes to see you again! (He bends down as if to kiss her, but, struck by a sudden fear, hesitates, straightens himself, and shamed by the understanding in Eileen's eyes, grows red and stammers confusedly.) How are you now? Sure it's the picture of health you're lookin'.

(Eileen sighs and turns her eyes away from him with a resigned sadness.)

MRS. BRENNAN. What are you standin' there for like a stick, Mary? Haven't you a word to say to your sister?

EILEEN (twisting her head around and seeing Mary for the first time—with a glad cry). Mary! I—why, I didn't see you before! Come here.

(Mary approaches gingerly with apprehensive side glances at Mrs. Brennan, who watches her grimly. Eileen's arms reach out for her hungrily. She grasps her about the waist and seems trying to press the unwilling child to her breast.)

MARY (fidgeting nervously—suddenly in a frightened whine). Let me go! (Eileen releases her, looks at her face dazedly for a second, then falls back limply with a little moan and shuts her eyes. Mary, who has stepped back a pace, remains fixed there as if fascinated with fright by her sister's face. She stammers.) Eileen—you look so—so funny.

EILEEN (without opening her eyes—in a dead voice). You, too! I never thought you—— Go away, please.

MRS. BRENNAN (with satisfaction). Come here to me, Mary, and don't be botherin' your sister.

(Mary avoids her step-mother, but retreats to the far end of the porch where she stands shrunk back against the wall, her eyes fixed on Eileen with the same fascinated horror.)

CARMODY (after an uncomfortable pause, forcing himself to speak). Is the pain bad, Eileen?

EILEEN (dully—without opening her eyes). There's no pain. (There is another pause—then she murmurs indifferently.) There are chairs in the room you can bring out if you want to sit down.

MRS. BRENNAN (sharply). We've not time to be sittin'. We've the train back to catch.

EILEEN (in the same lifeless voice). It's a disagreeable trip. I'm sorry you had to come.

CARMODY (fighting against an oppression he cannot understand, bursts into a flood of words). Don't be talking of the trip. Sure we're glad to take it to get a sight of you. It's three months since I've had a look at you, and I was anxious. Why haven't you written a line to us? You could do that without trouble, surely. Don't you ever think of us at all any more? (He waits for an answer, but Eileen remains silent with her eyes closed. Carmody starts to walk up and down, talking with an air of desperation.) You're not asking a bit of news from home. I'm thinkin' the people out here have taken all the thought of us out of your head. We're all well, thank God. I've another good job on the streets from Murphy and one that'll last a long time, praise be! I'm needin' it surely, with all the expenses—but no matter. Billy had a raise from his old skinflint of a boss a month back. He's gettin' seven a week now and proud as a turkey. He was comin' out with us to-day, but he'd a date with his girl. Sure, he's got a girl now, the young bucko! What d'you think of him? It's old Malloy's girl he's after—the pop-eyed one with glasses, you remember—as ugly as a blind sheep, only he don't think so. He said to give you his love. (Eileen stirs and sighs wearily, a frown appearing for an instant on her forehead.) And Tom and Nora was comin' out too, but Father Fitz had some doin's or other up to the school, and he told them to be there, so they wouldn't come with us, but they sent their love to you, too. They're growin' so big you'd not know them. Tom's no good at the school. He's like Billy was. I've had to take the strap to him often. He's always playin' hooky and roamin' the streets. And Nora. (With pride.) There's the divil for you! Up to everything she is and no holdin' her high spirits. As pretty as a picture, and the smartest girl in her school, Father Fitz says. Am I lyin', Maggie?

MRS. BRENNAN (grudgingly). She's smart enough—and too free with her smartness.

CARMODY (pleased). Ah, don't be talkin'! She'll know more than the lot of us before she's grown even. (He pauses in his walk and stares down at Eileen, frowning.) Are you sick, Eileen, that you're keepin' your eyes shut without a word out of you?

EILEEN (wearily). No. I'm tired, that's all.

CARMODY (resuming his walk). And who else is there, let me think? Oh, Mary—she's the same as ever, you can see for yourself.

EILEEN (bitterly). The same? Oh, no!

CARMODY. She's grown, you mean? I suppose. You'd notice, not seeing her so long?

(He can think of nothing else to say, but walks up and down with a restless, uneasy expression.)

MRS. BRENNAN (sharply). What time is it gettin'?

CARMODY (fumbles for his watch). Half-past four, a bit after.

MRS. BRENNAN. We'll have to leave soon. It's a long jaunt down that hill in that buggy.

(She catches his eye and makes violent signs to him to tell Eileen what he has come to tell.)

CARMODY (after an uncertain pause—clenching his fists and clearing his throat). Eileen.

EILEEN. Yes.

CARMODY (irritably). Can't you open your eyes on me? It's like talkin' to myself I am.

EILEEN (looking at him—dully). What is it?

CARMODY (stammering—avoiding her glance). It's this, Eileen—me and Maggie—Mrs. Brennan, that is—we——

EILEEN (without surprise). You're going to marry her?

CARMODY (with an effort). Not goin' to. It's done.

EILEEN (without a trace of feeling). Oh, so you've been married already?

(Without further comment, she closes her eyes.)

CARMODY. Two weeks back we were, by Father Fitz.

(He stands staring down at his daughter, irritated, perplexed and confounded by her silence, looking as if he longed to shake her.)

MRS. BRENNAN (angry at the lack of enthusiasm shown by Eileen). Let us get out of this, Bill. We're not wanted, that's plain as the nose on your face. It's little she's caring about you, and little thanks she has for all you've done for her and the money you've spent.

CARMODY (with a note of pleading). Is that a proper way to be treatin' your father, Eileen, after what I've told you? Have you no heart in you at all? Is it nothin' to you you've a good, kind woman now for mother?

EILEEN (fiercely, her eyes flashing open on him). No, no! Never!

MRS. BRENNAN (plucking at Carmody's elbow. He stands looking at Eileen helplessly, his mouth open, a guilty flush spreading over his face). Come out of here, you big fool, you! Is it to listen to insults to your livin' wife you're waiting? Am I to be tormented and you never raise a hand to stop her?

CARMODY (turning on her threateningly). Will you shut your gab?

EILEEN (with a moan). Oh, go away, Father! Please! Take her away!

MRS. BRENNAN (pulling at his arm). Take me away this second or I'll go on without you and never speak again to you till the day I die!

CARMODY (pushes her violently away from him—his fist uplifted). Shut your gab, I'm saying!

MRS. BRENNAN. The divil mend you and yours then! I'm leavin' you. (She starts for the door.)

CARMODY (hastily). Wait a bit, Maggie. I'm comin'. (She goes into the room, slamming the door, but once inside she stands still, trying to listen. Carmody glares down at his daughter's pale twitching face with the closed eyes. Finally he croaks in a whining tone of fear.) Is your last word a cruel one to me this day, Eileen?

(She remains silent. His face darkens. He turns and strides out of the door. Mary darts after him with a frightened cry of "Papa." Eileen covers her face with her hands and a shudder of relief runs over her body.)

MRS. BRENNAN (as Carmody enters the room—in a mollified tone). So you've come, have you? Let's go, then? (Carmody stands looking at her in silence, his expression full of gloomy rage. She bursts out impatiently.) Are you comin' or are you goin' back to her? (She grabs Mary's arm and pushes her towards, the door to the hall.) Are you comin' or not, I'm askin'?

CARMODY (sombrely—as if to himself). There's something wrong in the whole of this—that I can't make out. (With sudden fury he brandishes his fists as though defying someone and growls threateningly.) And I'll get drunk this night—dead, rotten drunk! (He seems to detect disapproval in Mrs. Brennan's face, for he shakes his fist at her and repeats like a solemn oath.) I'll get drunk this night, I'm sayin'! I'll get drunk if my soul roasts for it—and no one in the whole world is strong enough to stop me!

(Mrs. Brennan turns from him with a disgusted shrug of her shoulders and hustles Mary out of the door. Carmody, after a second's pause, follows them. Eileen lies still, looking out into the woods with empty, desolate eyes. Miss Howard comes into the room from the hall and goes to the porch, carrying a glass of milk in her hand.)

MISS HOWARD. Here's your diet, Eileen. I forgot it until just now. Sundays are awful days, aren't they? They get me all mixed up in my work, with all these visitors around. Did you have a nice visit with your folks?

EILEEN (forcing a smile). Yes.

MISS HOWARD. You look worn out. I hope they didn't worry you over home affairs?

EILEEN. No.

(She sips her milk and sets it back on the table with a shudder of disgust.)

MISS HOWARD (with a smile). What a face! You'd think you were taking poison.

EILEEN. I hate it! (With deep passion.) I wish it was poison!

MISS HOWARD (jokingly). Oh, come now! That isn't a nice way to feel on the Sabbath. (With a meaning smile.) I've some news that'll cheer you up, I bet. (Archly.) Guess who's here on a visit?

EILEEN (startled—in a frightened whisper). Who?

MISS HOWARD. Mr. Murray. (Eileen closes her eyes wincingly for a moment and a shadow of pain comes over her face.) He just came about the time your folks did. I saw him for a moment, not to speak to. He was going to the main building—to see Doctor Stanton, I suppose. (Beaming—with a certain curiosity.) What do you think of that for news?

EILEEN (trying to conceal her agitation and assume a casual tone). He must have come to be examined.

MISS HOWARD (with a meaning laugh). Oh, I'd hardly say that was his main reason. He does look much thinner and very tired, though. I suppose he's been working too hard. (In business-like tones.) Well, I've got to get back on the job. (She turns to the door calling back jokingly.) He'll be in to see you, of course, so look your prettiest.

(She goes out and shuts the door to the porch. Eileen gives a frightened gasp and struggles up in bed as if she wanted to call the nurse to return. Then she lies back in a state of great nervous excitement, twisting her head with eager, fearful glances towards the door, listening, clasping and unclasping her thin fingers on the white spread. As Miss Howard walks across the room to the hall door, it is opened and Stephen Murray enters. A great change is visible in his face. It is much thinner and the former healthy tan has faded to a sallow pallor. Puffy shadows of sleeplessness and dissipation are marked under his heavy-lidded eyes. He is dressed in a well-fitting, expensive dark suit, a white shirt with a soft collar and bright-coloured tie.)

MISS HOWARD (with pleased surprise, holding out her hand). Hello, Mr. Murray.

MURRAY (shaking her hand—with a forced pleasantness). How are you, Miss Howard?

MISS HOWARD. Fine as ever. It certainly looks natural to see you around here again—not that I hope you're here to stay, though. (With a smile.) I suppose you're on your way to Eileen now. Well, I won't keep you. I've stacks of work to do. (She opens the hall door. He starts for the porch.) Oh, I was forgetting—Congratulations! I've read those stories—all of us have. They're great. We're all so proud of you. You're one of our graduates, you know.

MURRAY (indifferently). Oh,—that stuff.

MISS HOWARD (gaily). Don't be so modest. Well, see you later, I hope.

MURRAY. Yes. Doctor Stanton invited me to stay for supper and I may——

MISS HOWARD. Fine! Be sure to!

(She goes out. Murray walks to porch door and steps out. He finds Eileen's eyes waiting for him. As their eyes meet she gasps involuntarily and he stops short in his tracks. For a moment they remain looking at each other in silence.)

EILEEN (dropping her eyes—faintly). Stephen.

MURRAY (much moved, strides to her bedside and takes her hands awkwardly). Eileen. (Then after a second's pause, in which he searches her face and is shocked by the change illness has made—anxiously.) How are you feeling, Eileen? (He grows confused by her gaze and his eyes shift from hers, which search his face with wild yearning.)

EILEEN (forcing a smile). Oh, I'm all right. (Eagerly.) But you, Stephen? How are you? (Excitedly.) Oh, it's good to see you again! (Her eyes continue fixed on his face pleadingly, questioningly.)

MURRAY (haltingly). And it's sure great to see you again, Eileen. (He releases her hand and turns away.) And I'm fine and dandy. I look a little done up, I guess, but that's only the result of too much New York.

(Eileen, sensing from his manner that whatever she has hoped for from his visit is not to be, sinks back on the pillows, shutting her eyes hopelessly, and cannot control a sigh of pain.)

MURRAY (turning to her anxiously). What's the matter, Eileen? You're not in pain, are you?

EILEEN (wearily). No.

MURRAY. You haven't been feeling badly lately, have you? Your letters suddenly stopped—not a line for the past three weeks—and I——

EILEEN (bitterly). I got tired of writing and never getting any answer, Stephen.

MURRAY (shame-faced). Come, Eileen, it wasn't as bad as that. You'd think I never—and I did write, didn't I?

EILEEN. Right after you left here, you did, Stephen. Lately——

MURRAY. I'm sorry, Eileen. It wasn't that I didn't mean to—but—in New York it's so hard. You start to do one thing and something else interrupts you. You never seem to get any one thing done when it ought to be. You can understand that, can't you, Eileen?

EILEEN (sadly). Yes. I understand everything now.

MURRAY (offended). What do you mean by everything? You said that so strangely. You mean you don't believe—— (But she remains silent with her eyes shut. He frowns and takes to pacing up and down beside the bed.) Why have they got you stuck out here on this isolation porch, Eileen?

EILEEN (dully). There was no room on the main porch, I suppose.

MURRAY. You never mentioned in any of your letters——

EILEEN. It's not very cheerful to get letters full of sickness. I wouldn't like to, I know.

MURRAY (hurt). That isn't fair, Eileen. You know I—— How long have you been back in the Infirmary?

EILEEN. About a month.

MURRAY (shocked). A month! But you were up and about—on exercise, weren't you—before that?

EILEEN. No. I had to stay in bed while I was at the cottage.

MURRAY. You mean—ever since that time they sent you back—the day before I left?

EILEEN. Yes.

MURRAY. But I thought from the cheery tone of your letters that you were——

EILEEN (uneasily). Getting better? I am, Stephen. I'm strong enough to be up now, but Doctor Stanton wants me to take a good long rest this time so that when I do get up again I'll be sure—— (She breaks off impatiently.) But don't let's talk about it. I'm all right. (Murray glances down at her face worriedly. She changes the subject.) You've been over to see Doctor Stanton, haven't you?

MURRAY. Yes.

EILEEN. Did he examine you?

MURRAY. Yes. (Carelessly.) Oh, he found me O.K. I'm fine and dandy, as I said before.

EILEEN. I'm glad, Stephen. (After a pause.) Tell about yourself—what you've been doing. You've written a lot lately, haven't you?

MURRAY (frowning). No. I haven't been able to get down to it—somehow. There's so little time to yourself once you get to know people in New York. The sale of the stories you typed put me on easy street as far as money goes, so I've felt no need—— (He laughs weakly.) I guess I'm one of those who have to get down to hard pan before they get the kick to drive them to hard work.

EILEEN (surprised). Was it hard work writing them up here? You used to seem so happy just in doing them.

MURRAY. I was—happier than I've been before or afterwards. (Cynically.) But—I don't know—it was a new game to me then and I was chuck full of illusions about the glory of it. (He laughs half-heartedly.) Now I'm hardly a bit more enthusiastic over it than I used to be over newspaper work. It's like everything else, I guess. When you've got it, you find you don't want it.

EILEEN (looking at him wonderingly—disturbed). But isn't just the writing itself worth while?

MURRAY (as if suddenly ashamed of himself—quickly). Yes. Of course it is. I'm talking like a fool. I'm sore at everything because I'm dissatisfied with my own cussedness and laziness—and I want to pass the buck. (With a smile of cheerful confidence.) It's only a fit. I'll come out of it all right and get down to brass tacks again.

EILEEN (with an encouraging smile). That's the way you ought to feel. It'd be wrong—I've read the two stories that have come out so far over and over. They're fine, I think. Every line in them sounds like you, and at the same time sounds natural and like people and things you see every day. Everybody thinks they're fine, Stephen.

MURRAY (pleased, but pretending cynicism). Then they must be rotten. (Then with self-assurance.) Well, I've plenty more of those stories in my head. Every time I think of my home town there seems to be a new story in someone I've known there. (Spiritedly.) Oh, I'll pound them out some time when the spirit moves; and I'll make them so much better than what I've done so far, you won't recognise them. I feel it's in me to do it. (Smiling.) Darn it, do you know just talking about it makes me feel as if I could sit right down now and start in on one. Is it the fact I've worked here before—or is it seeing you, Eileen. (Gratefully.) I really believe it's you. I haven't forgotten how you helped me before.

EILEEN (in a tone of pain). Don't, Stephen. I didn't do anything.

MURRAY (eagerly). Yes, you did. You made it possible. I can't tell you what a help you were. And since I've left the San, I've looked forward to your letters to boost up my spirits. When I felt down in the mouth over my own idiocy, I used to re-read them, and they always were good medicine. I can't tell you how grateful I've felt, honestly!

EILEEN (faintly). You're kind to say so, Stephen—but it was nothing, really.

MURRAY. And I can't tell you how I've missed those letters for the past three weeks. They left a big hole in things. I was worried about you—not having heard a word. (With a smile.) So I came to look you up.

EILEEN (faintly. Forcing an answering smile). Well, you see now I'm all right.

MURRAY (concealing his doubt). Yes, of course you are. Only I'd a darn sight rather see you up and about. We could take a walk, then—through the woods. (A wince of pain shadows Eileen's face. She closes her eyes. Murray continues softly, after a pause.) You haven't forgotten that last night—out there—Eileen?

EILEEN (her lips trembling—trying to force a laugh). Please don't remind me of that, Stephen. I was so silly and so sick, too. My temp was so high it must have made me—completely crazy—or I'd never dreamed of doing such a stupid thing. My head must have been full of wheels because I don't remember anything I did or said, hardly.

MURRAY (his pride taken down a peg by this—in a hurt tone). Oh! Well—I haven't forgotten and I never will, Eileen. (Then his face clears up as if a weight had been taken off his conscience.) Well—I rather thought you wouldn't take it seriously—afterwards. You were all up in the air that night. And you never mentioned it in your letters——

EILEEN (pleadingly). Don't talk about it! Forget it ever happened. It makes me feel—(with a half-hysterical laugh)—like a fool!

MURRAY (worried). All right, Eileen. I won't. Don't get worked up over nothing. That isn't resting, you know. (Looking down at her closed eyes—solicitously.) Perhaps all my talking has tired you out? Do you feel done up? Why don't you try and take a nap now?

EILEEN (dully). Yes, I'd like to sleep.

MURRAY (clasps her hands gently). I'll leave you then, I'll drop back to say good-bye and stay awhile before I go. I won't leave until the last train. (As she doesn't answer.) Do you hear, Eileen?

EILEEN (weakly). Yes. You'll come back—to say good-bye.

MURRAY. Yes. I'll be back sure.

(He presses her hand and after a kindly glance of sympathy down at her face, tiptoes to the door and goes into the room, shutting the door behind him. When she hears the door shut Eileen struggles up in bed and stretches her arms after him with an agonised sob "Stephen!" She hides her face in her hands and sobs brokenly. Murray walks across to the hall door and is about to go out when the door is opened and Miss Gilpin enters.)

MISS GILPIN (hurriedly). How do you do, Mr. Murray. Doctor Stanton just told me you were here.

MURRAY (as they shake hands—smiling). How are you, Miss Gilpin?

MISS GILPIN. He said he'd examined you, and that you were O.K. I'm glad. (Glancing at him keenly.) You've been talking to Eileen?

MURRAY. Just left her this second. She wanted to sleep for a while.

MISS GILPIN (wonderingly). Sleep? (Then hurriedly.) It's too bad. I wish I'd known you were here sooner. I wanted very much to talk to you before you saw Eileen. You see, I knew you'd pay us a visit some time. (With a worried smile.) I still think I ought to have a talk with you.

MURRAY. Certainly, Miss Gilpin.

MISS GILPIN (takes a chair and places it near the hall door). Sit down. She can't hear us here. Goodness knows this is hardly the place for confidences, but there are visitors all over and it'll have to do. Did you close the door tightly? She mustn't hear me above all. (She goes to the porch door and peeps out for a moment; then comes back to him with flashing eyes.) She's crying! What have you been saying to her? Oh, it's too late, I know! The fools shouldn't have permitted you to see her before I—— What has happened out there? Tell me! I must know.

MURRAY (stammering). Happened? Nothing. She's crying? Why, Miss Gilpin—you know I wouldn't hurt her for worlds.

MISS GILPIN (more calmly). Intentionally. I know you wouldn't. But something has happened. (Then briskly.) We're talking at cross purposes. Since you don't seem inclined to confide in me, I'll have to in you. You noticed how badly she looks, didn't you?

MURRAY. Yes, I did.

MISS GILPIN (gravely). She's been going down hill steadily—(meaningly)—ever since you left. She's in a very serious state, let me impress you with that. We've all loved her, and felt so sorry for her and admired her spirit so—that's the only reason she's been allowed to stay here so long after her time. We've kept hoping she'd start to pick up—in another day—in another week. But now that's all over. Doctor Stanton has given up hope of her improving here, and her father is unwilling to pay for her elsewhere now he knows there's a cheaper place—the State Farm. So she's to be sent there in a day or so.

MURRAY (springing to his feet—horrified). To the State Farm!

MISS GILPIN. Her time here is long past. You know the rule—and she isn't getting better.

MURRAY (appalled). That means——!

MISS GILPIN (forcibly). Death! That's what it means for her!

MURRAY (stunned). Good God, I never dreamed——

MISS GILPIN. With others it might be different. They might improve under changed surroundings. In her case, it's certain. She'll die. And it wouldn't do any good to keep her here, either. She'd die here. She'll die anywhere. She'll die because lately she's given up hope, she hasn't wanted to live any more. She's let herself go—and now it's too late.

MURRAY. Too late? You mean there's no chance—now? (Miss Gilpin nods. Murray is overwhelmed—after a pause—stammering.) Isn't there—anything—we can do?

MISS GILPIN (sadly). I don't know. I should have talked to you before you—— You see, she's seen you now. She knows. (As he looks mystified she continues slowly.) I suppose you know that Eileen loves you, don't you?

MURRAY (as if defending himself against an accusation—with confused alarm). No—Miss Gilpin. You're wrong, honestly. She may have felt something like that—once—but that was long ago before I left the San.

She's forgotten all about it since, I know she has. (Miss Gilpin smiles bitterly.) Why, she never even alluded to it in any of her letters—all these months.

MISS GILPIN. Did you in yours?

MURRAY. No, of course not. You don't understand. Why—just now—she said that part of it had all been so silly she felt she'd acted like a fool and didn't ever want to be reminded of it.

MISS GILPIN. She saw that you didn't love her—any more than you did in the days before you left. Oh, I used to watch you then. I sensed what was going on between you. I would have stopped it then out of pity for her, if I could have, if I didn't know that any interference would only make matters worse. And then I thought that it might be only a surface affair—that after you were gone it would end for her. (She sighs—then after a pause.) You'll have to forgive me for speaking to you so boldly on a delicate subject. But, don't you see, it's for her sake. I love Eileen. We all do. (Averting her eyes from his—in a low voice.) I know how Eileen feels, Mr. Murray. Once—a long time ago—I suffered as she is suffering—from this same mistake. But I had resources to fall back upon that Eileen hasn't got—a family who loved me and understood—friends—so I pulled through. But it spoiled my life for a long time. (Looking at him again and forcing a smile.) So I feel that perhaps I have a right to speak for Eileen who has no one else.

MURRAY (huskily—much moved). Say anything to me you like, Miss Gilpin.

MISS GILPIN (after a pause—sadly). You don't love her—do you?

MURRAY. No—I—I don't believe I've ever thought much of loving anyone—that way.

MISS GILPIN (sadly). Oh, it's too late, I'm afraid. If we had only had this talk before you had seen her! I meant to talk to you frankly and if I found out you didn't love Eileen—there was always the forlorn hope that you might—I was going to tell you not to see her, for her sake—not to let her face the truth. For I am sure she continued to hope in spite of everything, and always would—to the end—if she didn't see you. I was going to implore you to stay away, to write her letters that would encourage her hope, and in that way she would never learn the truth. I thought of writing you all this—but—it's so delicate a matter—I didn't have the courage. (With intense grief.) And now Doctor Stanton's decision to send her away makes everything doubly hard. When she knows that—she will throw everything that holds her to life—out of the window! And think of it—her dying there alone!

MURRAY (very pale). Don't! That shan't happen. I can at least save her from that. I have money enough—I'll make more—to send her to any place you think——

MISS GILPIN. That is something—but it doesn't touch the source of her unhappiness. If there were only some way to make her happy in the little time that is left to her! She has suffered so much through you. Oh, Mr. Murray, can't you tell her you love her?

MURRAY (after a pause—slowly). But she'll never believe me, I'm afraid, now.

MISS GILPIN (eagerly). But you must make her believe! And you must ask her to marry you. If you're engaged it will give you the right in her eyes to take her away. You can take her to some private San. There's a small place, but a very good one, at White Lake. It's not too expensive, and it's a beautiful spot, out of the world, and you can live and work near by. And she'll be happy to the very last. Don't you think that's something—the best you have—the best you can give in return for her love for you?

MURRAY (slowly—deeply moved). Yes. (Then determinedly.) But I won't go into this thing by halves. It isn't fair to her. I'm going to marry her—yes, I mean it. I owe her that if it will make her happy. But to ask her without really meaning it—knowing she—no, I can't do that.

MISS GILPIN (with a sad smile). I'm glad you feel that way. It shouldn't be hard now for you to convince her. But I know Eileen. She will never consent—for your sake—until she is well again. And stop and think, Mr. Murray. Even if she did consent to marry you right now the shock—the excitement—it would be suicide for her. I would have to warn her against it myself; and you wouldn't propose it if you knew the danger to her in her present condition. She hasn't long to live, at best. I've talked with Dr. Stanton. I know. God knows I would be the first one to hold out hope if there was any. There isn't. It's merely a case of prolonging the short time left to her and making it happy. You must bear that in mind—as a fact!

MURRAY (dully). All right. I'll remember. But it's hell to realise—— (He turns suddenly towards the porch door.) I'll go out to her now while I feel—that—yes, I know I can make her believe me now.

MISS GILPIN. You'll tell me—later on?

MURRAY. Yes. (He opens the door to the porch and goes out. Miss Gilpin stands for a moment looking after him worriedly. Then she sighs helplessly and goes out to the hall. Murray steps noiselessly out on the porch. Eileen is lying motionless with her eyes closed. Murray stands looking at her, his face showing the emotional stress he is under, a great pitying tenderness in his eyes. Then he seems to come to a revealing decision on what is best to do for he tiptoes to the bedside and bending down with a quick movement, takes her in his arms and kisses her.) Eileen!

EILEEN (startled at first, resists automatically for a moment). Stephen! (Then she succumbs and lies back in his arms with a happy sigh, putting both hands to the sides of his face and staring up at him adoringly.) Stephen, dear!

MURRAY (quickly questioning her before she can question him). You were fibbing—about that night—weren't you? You do love me, don't you, Eileen?

EILEEN (breathlessly). Yes—I—but you, Stephen—you don't love me. (She makes a movement as if to escape from his embrace.)

MURRAY (genuinely moved—with tender reassurance). Why do you suppose I came up here if not to tell you I did? But they warned me—Miss Gilpin—that you were still weak and that I mustn't excite you in any way. And I—I didn't want—but I had to come back and tell you in spite of them.

EILEEN (convinced—with a happy laugh). And is that why you acted so strange—and cold? Aren't they silly to tell you that! As if being happy could hurt me! Why, it's just that, just you I've needed!

MURRAY (his voice trembling). And you'll marry me, Eileen?

EILEEN (a shadow of doubt crossing her face momentarily). Are you sure—you want me, Stephen?

MURRAY (a lump in his throat—huskily). Yes. I do want you, Eileen.

EILEEN (happily). Then I will—after I'm well again, of course. (She kisses him.)

MURRAY (chokingly). That won't be long now, Eileen.

EILEEN (joyously). No—not long—now that I'm happy for once in my life. I'll surprise you, Stephen, the way I'll pick up and grow fat and healthy. You won't know me in a month. How can you ever love such a skinny homely thing as I am now! (With a laugh.) I couldn't if I was a man—love such a fright.

MURRAY. Sssh!

EILEEN (confidently). But you'll see now. I'll make myself get well. We won't have to wait long, dear. And can't you move up to the town near here where you can see me every day, and you can work and I can help you with your stories just as I used to—and I'll soon be strong enough to do your typing again. (She laughs.) Listen to me—talking about helping you—as if they weren't all your own work, those blessed stories!—as if I had anything to do with it!

MURRAY (hoarsely). You had! You did! They're yours. (Trying to calm himself.) But you mustn't stay here, Eileen. You'll let me take you away, won't you?—to a better place—not far away—White Lake, it's called. There's a small private sanatorium there. Doctor Stanton says it's one of the best. And I'll live near by—it's a beautiful spot—and see you every day.

EILEEN (in the seventh heaven). And did you plan out all this for me beforehand, Stephen? (He nods with averted eyes. She kisses his hair.) You wonderful, kind dear! And it's a small place—this White Lake? Then we won't have so many people around to disturb us, will we? We'll be all to ourselves. And you ought to work so well up there. I know New York wasn't good for you—alone—without me. And I'll get well and strong so quick! And you say it's a beautiful place? (Intensely.) Oh, Stephen, any place in the world would be beautiful to me—if you were with me! (His face is hidden in the pillow beside her. She is suddenly startled by a muffled sob—anxiously.) Why—Stephen—you're—you're crying! (The tears start to her own eyes.)

MURRAY (raising his face which is this time alight with a passionate awakening—a revelation). Oh, I do love you, Eileen. I do! I love you, love you!

EILEEN (thrilled by the depth of his present sincerity—but with a teasing laugh). Why, you say that as if you'd just made the discovery, Stephen!

MURRAY. Oh, what does it matter, Eileen! I love you! Oh, what a blind, selfish ass I've been! I love you! You are my life—everything! I love you, Eileen! I do! I do! And we'll be married——

(Suddenly his face grows frozen with horror as he remembers the doom. For the first time the grey spectre of Death confronts him face to face as a menacing reality.)

EILEEN (terrified by the look in his eyes). What is it, Stephen? What——?

MURRAY (with a groan—protesting half-aloud in a strangled voice). No! No! It can't be——! My God! (He clutches her hands and hides his face in them.)

EILEEN (with a cry). Stephen! What is the matter? (Her face suddenly betrays apprehension, an intuitive sense of the truth.) Oh—Stephen——(Then with a childish whimper of terror.) Oh, Stephen, I'm going to die! I'm going to die!

MURRAY (lifting his tortured face—wildly). No!

EILEEN (her voice sinking to a dead, whisper). I'm going to die.

MURRAY (seizing her in his arms in a passionate frenzy and pressing his lips to hers). No, Eileen, no, my love, no! What are you saying? What could have made you think it? You—die? Why, of course, we're all going to die—but—Good God! What damned nonsense! You're getting well—every day. Everyone—Miss Gilpin—Stanton—everyone told me that. I swear before God, Eileen, they did! You're still weak, that's all. They said—it won't be long. You mustn't think that—not now.

EILEEN (miserably—unconvinced). But why did you look at me—that way—with that awful look in your eyes——?

(While she is speaking Miss Gilpin enters the room from the corridor. She appears worried, agitated. She hurries towards the porch, but stops inside the doorway, arrested by Murray's voice.)

MURRAY (takes Eileen by the shoulders and forces her to look into his eyes). I wasn't thinking about you then—— No, Eileen—not you. I didn't mean you—but me—yes, me! I couldn't tell you before. They'd warned me—not to excite you—and I knew that would—if you loved me.

EILEEN (staring at him with frightened amazement). You mean you—you're sick again?

MURRAY (desperately striving to convince her). Yes. I saw Stanton. I lied to you before—about that. It's come back on me, Eileen—you see how I look—I've let myself go. I don't know how to live without you, don't you see? And you'll—marry me now—without waiting—and help me to get well—you and I together—and not mind their lies—what they say to prevent you? You'll do that, Eileen?

EILEEN. I'll do anything for you—— And I'd be so happy—— (She breaks down.) But, Stephen, I'm so afraid. I'm all mixed up. Oh, Stephen, I don't know what to believe!

MISS GILPIN (who has been listening thunderstruck to Murray's wild pleading, at last summons up the determination to interfere—steps out on the porch—a tone of severe remonstrance). Mr. Murray!

MURRAY (starts to his feet with wild, bewildered eyes—confusedly). Oh—you—— (Miss Gilpin cannot restrain an exclamation of dismay as she sees his face wrung by despair. Eileen turns her head away with a little cry, as if she would hide her face in the bedclothes. A sudden fierce resolution lights up Murray's countenance—hoarsely.) You're just in the nick of time, Miss Gilpin! Eileen! Listen! You'll believe Miss Gilpin, won't you? She knows all about it. (Eileen turns her eyes questioningly on the bewildered nurse.)

MISS GILPIN. What——?

MURRAY (determinedly). Miss Gilpin, Doctor Stanton has spoken to you since he examined me. He must have told you the truth about me. Eileen doesn't believe me—when I tell her I've got T.B. again. She thinks—I don't know what. I know you're not supposed to, but can't you make an exception—in this case? Can't you tell Eileen the truth?

MISS GILPIN (stunned by being thus defiantly confronted—stammeringly). Mr. Murray! I—I—how can you ask——

MURRAY (quickly). Eileen has a right to know. She loves me—and I—I—love her! (He holds her eyes and speaks with a passion of sincerity that compels belief.) I love her, do you hear?

MISS GILPIN (falteringly). You—love—Eileen?

MURRAY. Yes! I do! (Entreatingly.) So—tell her—won't you?

MISS GILPIN (swallowing hard, her eyes full of pity and sorrow fixed on Eileen). Yes—Eileen—it's true. (She turns away slowly towards the door.)

EILEEN (with a little cry of alarmed concern, stretches out her hands to Murray protectingly). Poor Stephen—dear! (He grasps her hands and kisses them.)

MISS GILPIN (in a low voice). Mr. Murray. May I speak to you for a moment?

MURRAY (with a look of questioning defiance at her). Certainly.

MISS GILPIN (turns to Eileen with a forced smile). I won't steal him away for more than a moment, Eileen. (Eileen smiles happily.)

MURRAY (follows Miss Gilpin into the room. She leads him to the far end of the room near the door to the hall, after shutting the porch door carefully behind him. He looks at her defiantly). Well?

MISS GILPIN (in low agitated tones). What has happened? What is the meaning—I feel as if I may have done a great wrong to myself—to you—to her—by that lie. And yet—something impelled me.

MURRAY (moved). Don't regret it, Miss Gilpin! It has saved her—us. Oh, how can I explain what happened? I suddenly saw—how beautiful and sweet and good she is—how I couldn't bear the thought of life without her—her love—— That's all. (Determinedly.) She must marry me at once and I will take her away—the far West—any place Stanton thinks can help.

And she can take care of me—as she thinks—and I know she will grow well as I seem to grow well. Oh Miss Gilpin, don't you see? No half and half measures—no promises—no conditional engagements—can help us—help her. We love too much! (Fiercely, as if defying her.) But we'll win together. We can! We must! There are things your doctors cannot value—cannot know the strength of! (Exultantly.) You'll see! I'll make Eileen get well, I tell you! Happiness will cure! Love is stronger than—— (He suddenly breaks down before the pitying negation she cannot keep from her eyes. He sinks on a chair, shoulders bowed, face hidden in his hands, with a groan of despair.) Oh, why did you give me a hopeless hope?

MISS GILPIN (putting her hand on his shoulder—with tender compassion—sadly). Isn't everything we know—just that—when you think of it? (Her face lighting up with a consoling revelation.) But there must be something behind it—some promise of fulfilment,—somehow—somewhere—in the spirit of hope itself.

MURRAY (dully). Yes—but what do words mean to me now? (Then suddenly starting to his feet and flinging off her hand with disdainful strength—violently and almost insultingly.) What damned rot! I tell you we'll win! We must! Oh, I'm a fool to waste words on you! What can you know? Love isn't in the materia medica. Your predictions—all the verdicts of all the doctors—what do they matter to me? This is—beyond you! And we'll win in spite of you! (Scornfully.) How dare you use the word hopeless—as if it were the last! Come now, confess, damn it! There's always hope, isn't there? What do you know? Can you say you know anything?

MISS GILPIN (taken aback by his violence for a moment, finally bursts into a laugh of helplessness which is close to tears). I? I know nothing—absolutely nothing! God bless you both!

(She raises her handkerchief to her eyes and hurries out to the corridor without turning her head. Murray stands looking after her for a moment; then strides out to the porch.)

EILEEN (turning and greeting him with a shy smile of happiness as he comes and kneels by her bedside). Stephen! (He kisses her. She strokes his hair and continues in a tone of motherly, self-forgetting solicitude.) I'll have to look out for you, Stephen, won't I? From now on? And see that you rest so many hours a day—and drink your milk when I drink mine—and go to bed at nine sharp when I do—and obey everything I tell you—and——

THE CURTAIN FALLS

Milton Keynes UK
Ingram Content Group UK Ltd.
UKHW030956261124
451585UK00005B/720

9 789362 992024